Cover design by Sadie E. Nezich of Concord Consulting, LLC
Editing and formatting by Amanda E. Clark of Grammar Chic, Inc. - www.grammarchic.net

ISBN 978-1-4507-2858-4

Published by EDGE Publishing Company
8939 Sweetbriar St.
Manassas, VA 20110
(703)447-3780
www.edgepublishingcompany.com

Dedicated To

I would like to first dedicate this book to my wife, Arlean. You sacrificed everything for me at such a young age. I know it must have been hard to be cut off from your family at 13 and I have tried to fathom what this must have felt like for you. You gave up so much for me. I want you to know that you saved my life and my eternal soul by helping me part with my Mother's evil ways. I love you. You are my Angel.

I also would like to dedicate this book to my children, Randy W. Burt, Jr., Michael C. Burt, Ariel Burt, Jessica Burt, and my many grandchildren. You have all paid a price because of the acts committed by another. I hope this book finally helps you understand what went on and what it took for us to protect you….

I would also like to dedicate this to a teacher who influenced my life, Mrs. Walsh.

Thank You.

Published by EDGE Publishing Company
Manassas, VA
www.edgepublishingcompany.com

Fifth Commandment Atrocity

Randy Burt

EDGE Publishing Company
Manassas, VA
www.edgepublishingcompany.com

FOREWORD

Editor's Note

Working through the editorial and publishing process on this book was one that entailed Randy Burt to search through his memory bank and pull out and organize some of the most traumatic experiences of his life. The book was written to be as accurate as possible and was based on Randy's ability to remember and recount these situations from his firsthand experience. While every effort has been made to quote players in this story accurately, some statements, quotes, or thoughts may not be presented verbatim. The information in this book has been matched up to reflect accurate court records. The names of individuals involved in this book, with exception to Frances Burt, Walter Burt, Dennis Burt, Randy Burt, and Arlean Burt have been changed.

~ Amanda Clark, Editor
Fifth Commandment Atrocity

FOREWORD

Author's Note

The stories told in this book represent my ability to remember certain details growing up in my family's home from the time I was a child until the time when the majority of my family went to prison. Depending on the subject matter involved, as I recount a story, it might be because I witnessed it firsthand, overheard conversations regarding the subject matter, was told of a situation through hearsay of another family member or family friend, or because of actions that were witnessed by myself regarding those individuals involved. Some of these stories are backed up by police records and court documents. For instance, I know that certain members of my family, namely Dennis and Raymond, engaged in criminal activity. While I did not witness the criminal activity firsthand, both were prosecuted for their crimes.

I also mention some sensitive information regarding one subject, namely the rape of various women in, or associated with the Burt family. I know this information based upon the stories told to me by the victims and the eventual affidavits of the victims' statements that were entered into court proceedings. These statements were used to indict the guilty parties for their crimes against these women.

Furthermore, while my story does detail some criminal activity that includes shoplifting by various family members, I do not encourage anyone to take part in this activity or to believe that this book is a manual or a "how-to" book to mimic criminal behavior. In today's technologically advanced world, these methods simply would not work and anyone who believes they could get away with what I talk about is probably going to find themselves in trouble. Don't attempt to follow in the Burt family's footsteps.

Additionally, the methods discussed regarding the use of arson and the resulting insurance fraud should not be considered as a handbook for this type of crime. This is an illegal act of the highest criminal order and I highly encourage no one to ever consider this. It not only could result in incarceration, but also death.

Part I
Growing Up Burt

Finding a Voice

I was raised in Pawtucket and Cumberland, Rhode Island and my life never seemed spectacular or out of the ordinary growing up. I guess that's because all of the horrible things my family did just became a natural way of life. To me, at least until I hit the age where I was old enough to start to know any better, my childhood was somewhat normal. I had a father, a mother, two older brothers, a younger sister and a younger brother. From the outside looking in, anyone who didn't know the details would say that the Burts were a close-knit family because, from all appearances, we had a lot, we did a lot, we were wealthy and, in so many people's mind, people with money just weren't involved in the kind of large-scale, awe and shock-inspiring level of crime that we were behind closed doors. To them, we had it all-we had a large family home, took vacations in our motor home, had a summer house on a lake, and a Springer Spaniel dog. The Burts lived the life.

However, closer inspection would reveal a little more. My parents took in eight foster kids and adopted a daughter – one of whom they stole from her mother. The Burts had hired help, if you want to call being hired keeping two adults against their will in our basement. They ran a shoplifting ring, an arson-for-profit scheme, sexually abused many, and tortured all of us. That was my understanding of normal, I had no other family life to compare anything to. And the more the public learned about the details of what was going on in our house, the more we became public enemy #1. And for good reason, too.

When I say I was in the middle of it all, I mean that literally. I was lost in the shuffle of this family that grew and grew and added more layers of trauma with each passing year. From my vantage point in the middle I saw a lot—too much.

I was born to Walter and Frances Burt in 1966 and was raised in the suburbs of Providence, Rhode Island in a coercive and illicit family. In 1993 my parents, most of my siblings, some of their spouses and a few family associates were indicted on 158 counts of criminal charges by a Providence County Grand Jury. The charges and accusations ranged from kidnapping, to arson, to racketeering, to conspiracy and sexual assault. In 1994 my family received suspended sentences for the crimes they committed, in part due to my cooperation with the police and Grand Jury testimony. In 1994, I was set free from the hold my family had over me. I never did any prison time, but I am very much aware today that, in essence, I am serving a life sentence. I am guilty of bearing the name of my family.

I have tried to escape my past and at times, my identity. I have moved a few times to different states and started my life over – but no matter where I run, my history creeps up behind me. The story of the Burts just won't go away. In 2004, CBS aired a movie entitled "Family Sins" and claimed it was based on my family. In 2009, Lifetime re-aired the movie — the depiction of our life in that movie bared little resemblance to the one I lived.

I cannot run from my past any longer and I cannot stay silent. I will always be a Burt, but my past will no longer define me. It is time to set the record straight about who we were and what we did. I tell this story not for revenge or out of hatred of my family. I don't tell this story because I necessarily want to. I tell this because I need to. I need to tell it for my wife and for my children and grandchildren and for the generations to come. I need to set them free of this life sentence.

My children have been implicated by my past. They have received calls and hateful emails asking how their parents could do the things they did? Like they were somehow implicated and guilty by association. I refuse to let them live the way I have been forced to live. My children have no way to respond, they open their eyes wide and attempt to speak but lack the words to do it. I do not always have the answers they seek. It seems like a sad, weak excuse to tell them that it was impossible to resist what had become a "normal" way of life—the theft, the violence. It seems like it is not enough to tell them that while I am also guilty of some atrocious crimes, I felt that what I was doing was wrong. You see, my mother in particular never felt wrong. They took as much as they could get with her at the helm and, being unable to break free, I had no choice but to go along. We were, all of us kids, beaten into submission and driven to obedience through the machinations of one of the most cunning and bold criminals in modern times.

So I will speak for them. A voice needs to be given. No fictionalization for a genteel made for television audience is necessary. The truth is vital for my sake and the sake of my family.

I am not my past. My children are not my past. My grandchildren must understand what happened so this foul legacy can come to an end.

I am Randy Burt and this is my life story.

APPLES FALLING FROM TREES

How many times in my life have I heard a statement that went something along the lines of "the apple doesn't fall from the tree" and cringed, feeling shameful, saddened, helpless, and angry that I had been locked into something that I so desperately feel is not me. But from an outsider's perspective, since I was involved in a lot of the acts, most likely criminal in nature, which my parents devised, I am guilty. Therefore, I will always be the apple that didn't fall far from the tree. What people don't understand when they make their accusations and say that I should have gone to jail with the rest of that sad lot is that I, along with some others in my family and our extended network of friends and accomplices, didn't act on the principles of sheer evil—we did what we did because we didn't know any better. We had been raised to think that the abhorrent was normal—that the worst was always the standard. More importantly, we were raised to live in constant, pervasive fear of my mother, Frances Burt, the mastermind of more crimes than the police and their ranks of officers and investigators could have ever tallied.

We would try to hide in the bathroom from beatings; there was nothing that she wouldn't do to us. When it came to torturing us she was at her most creative. She'd stick our heads in the toilet—that was always the worst, most humiliating punishment. Another of the most horrible, and most creative, was when she would throw rice on the ground, make us kneel on it for an hour or two, and then beat us. It hurts beyond words, kneeling on rice. It's like kneeling on little pebbles, all for an hour or more at a time. And it's not like we ever dared to move.

My mom was also very protective of her stuff and we learned damn quick not to touch something that we weren't supposed to. The standard punishment for that little crime—and we all got it at one time or another—was watching and waiting in agony as the electric stove turned a bright hot, angry red-orange. Then she'd grab our fingers (her hands were always frightfully, almost manly strong) and wipe them against the stove's burning coil until we almost passed out. You could smell burning flesh in the kitchen when she would inflict that punishment.

But the worst thing about all of it is that you never knew when your time would come. That's because it didn't even take us doing anything wrong for her to snap and flip—grabbing our wrists, forcing us into whatever cruel idea struck her for that day.

These kinds of things happened on a regular basis. They were not isolated events yet there was also no timeframe. Anything— and I do mean anything— could have happened to any of us at any point in time. You just never knew; it was a crapshoot. For instance, I believe that she used the beatings as a way to vent her frustrations with whatever she had on her mind. She was famous for coming to my bedroom on the third floor, or into my brothers and sisters rooms, just to see what we were up to. If she found us laying around, doing nothing, she would dump out the dresser drawers and give us a time limit to clean it all up, and to make it just so. She would come back when time expired to inspect our handiwork. If we failed to get it just how she wanted it or if it wasn't all cleaned up when she entered the room, some form of beating would come. I don't know if she did this because she was just really crazy, or hell, maybe she was just bored. She was just a horrible, horrible woman. Those words alone are a joke when it comes to trying to explain life in the Burt family, but until you give me the chance to offer the details to back that assertion, those words will have to suffice.

I can't fathom the idea that the justice system ever allowed her to get out of jail — that was the biggest injustice to everyone; she should have died in jail just like the prosecutor said she was going to do.

And I tell you all of this not so that you feel sorry for me, not so that you find a way to forgive me, but so that you understand something very important. As you read on, you're going to see me as a guilty son of a bitch and it's true, there were times I was guilty of some things. But I did these things not out of the driving force of evil that guided my parents—my mom in particular, I did these things because fear ruled my life. We had been brainwashed. She wanted us to be scared to death of her yet still completely reliant on her. She wanted us to grovel, to become her slaves—and some of the kids (and adults, for that matter) were like this.

We wanted her, in some sick way, to accept us. And that, above all else and when coupled with crippling fear, explains more than I can hope to communicate, even in the length and breadth of this narrative.

What I am trying to say is that our family was not a family in the traditional sense of the world. Nor was it something as coherent as a criminal organization. It was a cult, plain and simple. For some cults, their religion is based on something higher than any individual, for my mother's cult (because make no mistake, she was our charismatic leader) the mode of worship was crime.

This criminal cult was made up of adopted and biological family members and then, as things really started to expand, of outsiders who were ushered into the fold and never allowed to look back at their old lives again. Ours was a cult under the leadership of a person with an unbelievable capacity to twist and manipulate. A person with the awful, uncanny ability to make everyone who came into her web unable to think clearly again, to remember just who they were before—this person was my own mother.

Before you read further, before you pass judgment on any of us who stayed in that family, remember Jonestown. Remember Waco. Because let me tell you, even if it wasn't a religion with Christ at the forefront, the religion of crime, money, greed, and sin was one that was pounded into all of us from the first day of our lives until it all finally unraveled. This was a religion to my family and the principles other religions are based on—mercy, kindness, higher powers—were meaningless. In this religion all that mattered was that you didn't look back, that you didn't leave the fold, and that you did exactly what Frances wanted.

Or else.

Just like the victims of other cults throughout history, anyone who wasn't born into the family or adopted at a young age into it, could also serve a function. Whether it was a boyfriend or girlfriend or outside party who came around the house, Queen Frances could use anyone and it was impossible to leave. She made everyone sever ties to their family and friends by force and coercion. She made everyone feel so small and pathetic that they ended up, without realizing, going to her for every little thing until they were utterly dependent on her for everything in life. She made us all slaves—it's just that some of us got an earlier start than others.

No Rhyme, No Reason

There is no excuse for anything my family did. I am tempted to say that both of my parents were born with a type of short-circuit in morality, humanity, and compassion. And they couldn't blame their behavior on the fact that they had kids because they were these people long before any of us entered the picture.

When we hear about people doing horrible things, especially to their own kids, we're too quick sometimes to overlook the fact that the person might just be heartless or evil and instead we try to look back in their past for something—anything—that might have sparked a rage so profound to justify sick or inhumane actions. Very often, especially with serial killers or people who just go off and snap one day, there is something, some critical event, that leads that person down a path of instability. And especially in our court systems, that makes us able to somehow justify the horror of the actions people commit. "Oh, well, yes, that person did murder kids, but did you hear about his childhood?" we say, but you know, someone's childhood or their past trauma doesn't always provide an answer.

I truly believe these days that two things lie at opposite ends of the spectrum. First, there are some people who are just born without the ability to feel—without the capability to experience empathy, sympathy, humanity. They are hollow people, empty in every sense outside of what their own, sometimes crippling desires fill them with. These people can be raised in the most standard, wholesome, happy household with a loving family and trauma-free youth and still, due to this major flaw, this omission of the soul, they can go on to be the most profoundly evil people in society.

On the other hand, I also believe that it is very much possible for people who grow up with significant trauma, especially after being raised by people who lack the capacity to experience care and human emotion in any meaningful way, to make it through. To get by and work things out without going off the deep end—without helplessly locking themselves into the same sick cycles of abuse that they themselves experienced.

So while I do believe that the way we are raised has significant bearing on who we become, I do not think it's the be-all and end-all source of who we are fundamentally. We are shaped and formed, but in the end, it is our decision, even if that decision comes later in our lives, to create ourselves. This is how I have tried to rationalize my own existence as Frances and Walter Burt's son. What I see now from a distance is a boy who was afraid for years to break away for fear of what it might mean—I was a person who wanted to fit in while at the same time wanting nothing more than to get away.

What I realized was that my guilt over some of the things I have done has been internalized—but I know that I can accept my responsibility and role in some acts that I am not proud of. I can forgive myself because I know that I did not do those things because I was somehow fundamentally evil, but because the way I was raised made things acceptable that were, by society's view, unacceptable—that I always knew and keenly felt were wrong, but knew that I was expected to go through with them anytime an opportunity presented itself.

I am not saying that I have an excuse for anything I did. But I am saying that pressure to act and behave a certain way within my family was heavily enforced through the use of beatings and torture. I am not saying that anything I ever did was justified because I was just being a good little soldier and was only carrying out orders from someone far more evil than I could ever imagine being. I can't say that—nothing is justified. What I am saying is that the clarity after being apart from them for so many years now has led me to see just how powerful our families can be in the formulation of identity and personality. Because with them gone, I got to know myself and found that I am not evil. I am a Burt and for this I will forever be sorry, but I am not evil. Evil is a strong word that really only can be applied to those hollow people—those who are born without basic but incredibly important human emotions. People like my mother, Frances Burt.

With my mom, people get flustered because they want to look for some rhyme or reason, anything at all, to explain how someone could be so consistently heartless and unfeeling. They want to see something that might have triggered a hatred so profound it never melted away and only grew stronger, more violent, more perverted in its intensity. People are bothered though, because look as they might, there are very few clues to help them in their armchair psychoanalysis. The fact is actually sickeningly simple—she just wasn't fully human.

I know that a lot of people want to try to reconstruct my mother's life, try to find some rhyme or reason behind her awful cruelty and heartless actions. Many people think that something truly traumatic and horrible must have happened to her when she was young, after all, something must have made it natural for her to treat children the way she did. The thing is, even though she rarely ever talked at all about her life in Panama and the time before she came with my dad to the States, nothing ever really made me think she was treated awfully or abused. But the one thing that I do think really did have an influence on her was the fact that her family was so damn poor.

The thing is though, most of the people who lived in or near her village were poor. She would not have known or seen another, more glamorous side to pine about and be sickly jealous about that I know of. Many years later, we all went to Panama to see the land of her birth, but there were no clues there. Nothing to indicate what could have given rise to such a monster. It was just poverty—extreme, dire poverty. And it was everywhere you looked. No flushing toilets, running water, nothing. People were dirty and many of them not in the best health, but they seemed like genuinely good people.

My only guess at this is to suggest that she was born hollow. That's the pure, sick simplicity of it. Where a heart or soul should be there is just empty space. To get by, empty people like this just fake concern and care enough to not draw attention to themselves and then, when they are on their own, they can use this skill of fake compassion to lure people into their webs of deceit, lies, and evil. Because I do feel that people like this, like Frances Burt, really do not feel anything. They cannot. Just like some people are born with birth defects like a missing arm, my mom was born missing a soul—a heart.

Back around the time when my mom's then-young family moved to the new house on Spring Street, my mom got the idea to move her mom, step-dad and her brother Daniel from Panama to America and place them in the cottage. This meant the family that had been in there before, the Travis family, had to leave to make room for this group of people, that until they arrived at our house, none of us knew much, if anything, about. I think my mom was excited to show off her wealth and while her mother and brother seemed impressed, in truth, I think they didn't quite know what to make of the whole situation. The world that they came from—the same one that my mother grew up in and lived in before she met my dad—was dramatically different from the one they were part of now. For my maternal grandmother and for mom's brother, having a roof over their heads, running water, and the basic electrical appliances were a source of amazement. Seeing the way she lived, with her red carpets (these ended up being everywhere in our houses since she considered them a sign of class), they were astounded, for sure.

I am not quite sure what was going through her mind when she brought them from Panama. I never got the impression that there was any kind of particular love for these people—my mom really didn't love anyone but herself. I have wondered for some time, in fact, where the selfish motivation was in her decision to use her own money. Doing something selfless just wasn't in my mom's nature. It still mystifies me.

Things did turn sour and it didn't take long. The situation just seemed to naturally lend itself to tension. I think my mom wanted these people to look to her as some kind of saintly queen—as someone who saved them from poverty. I think she felt that way because she had probably always grown up wanting such a saint—someone to rescue her from her poor life of little means. She thought she found that person in my father when she first met him during his stint in the military in Panama, but as she reminded him for years and years after, she never loved him and he'd failed miserably at living up to her ideal. In her mind, she had to do everything herself. It was very difficult living up to Frances Burt's expectations, although being wealthy was by itself, a good start.

From what she's always said about things, I have no idea what she saw in my dad to begin with. She always talked about how ugly he was—right to his face. By the time I was old enough to think about the dynamics of my parents' relationship, it seemed to me, and my wife Arlean too, that my dad was just so beaten down that he took whatever she threw at him. He'd given up trying to change her and just found things to do—his ways of keeping her happy. Unfortunately for a lot of the foster girls in the house, Nadine, and all of the female tenants he tried to trade sex for rent, the hobbies that kept him out of her hair were anything but innocuous. I believe this because of the information provided by the victims, the affidavits provided to the police and court system and the court proceedings that were taken against guilty parties. I don't think he really loved her either—it was just a weird sort of mutually beneficial arrangement rather than a loving marriage. Then again, I don't get the impression that my parents were the type to ever value everyday romance. Especially my mom.

A major lawsuit, fraudulent of course, was what allowed my parents to buy that 16-room mansion on Spring Street with the cottage in back that my maternal grandmother and other members of my mom's family—none of whom spoke any real English—ended up living in. The whole time leading up to the purchase of the huge, awful old place, my dad was working for a slaughterhouse. He didn't really have anything to do with the meat itself outside of driving trucks around for the company out to different markets in and around the city. Naturally, he stole a lot of the meat he was supposed to be delivering, so much so that he had a big hand in that company going out of business. My family had a real knack of forcing once solid, long-running businesses right into bankruptcy and playing an integral role in helping them close their doors permanently. So after the slaughterhouse closed down, dad went to work for this convenience store. And as was custom, after working for them for a while and employing all of his friends and family members, he robbed them blind—almost to the point of going under.

The whole situation at this company was starting to attract some unwanted attention—dad knew that they were onto him. He had to knock off the more outright theft and work the place over from another, more subtle angle. His solution ended up being ridiculously easy and he scored a mega-settlement after merely going in early, knocking over a bunch of shelves, laying a ladder in the pile, and making it look like he was changing a bulb before he fell. So with this mess in place, all he had to do was wait for some unsuspecting person to walk through the door to see him, artfully sprawled out and faking a howl of pain because of what was supposed to be a back injury. This insurance scam never got old to my parents and my dad, in particular, used this one many, many times.

This was all, of course, before the advent of security cameras and national databases to keep track of the names and information of people who seem to file a suspicious number of claims. But still, I am astounded that he—and my mom and all of her fraud—were able to skate along as easily as they did for as long as they did. Astounded.

I guess that the point I'm trying to make here is that there is no real rhyme or reason when it comes to my family. My mom was the worst offender but my dad was bad too—they schemed all the time. They looked for the easiest, quickest ways to get rich and didn't give any kind of thought to what their gains might have cost other people. It started before we were born and got sicker and more complex as time went on. They annihilated their own families, drove everyone but the weakest of us away, and created a world of lies, guilt, sin and sickness.

BACK TO THE START OF MY LIFE...

I stood, confused and frightened, at the top landing of the basement stairs, watching as the man who lived on the third floor of my parents' building stormed the house in search of my parents. It wasn't just him this time; his son came with him and he wasn't barehanded—through my young eyes I saw that he was wielding an axe. He had a wild spark in his eyes I will never forget.

At the age of four I couldn't have known what the argument was really about or why the man with the axe suddenly turned on my mother, bringing the rusty blade down on her hand and nearly severing two of her fingers. I felt helpless as I watched my mother crumple on the stairs, holding her mangled hand and crying in pain and anger, crying out for my father. Not so much simply so he could help her, as much as that she knew she was down and revenge and violence was needed.

My father came running at the sound of struggle and screams and spotted my mother, who was hunched over and seething in a pool of blood. She held up the remains of her hand to show the two fingers that were only barely still attached by sinew. The vicious, agonized expression on her face was enough to send him into action. His eyes glazed over; he was in the mode—the one that would make him capable of anything, even murdering whoever it was that dared take an axe to his wife— and in his building, no less. My father barked at my mother to go and call the police and sounded a warning out to my older brothers, then he stormed into the basement, which was where my mother told them the men had gone.

From my spot on the basement landing, which by then was slick with my mother's blood, I grimly watched as a scene I could not look away from unfolded before me. Without a fore-thought, my father attacked the men with full force, wrestling and punching the two men as my brother Dennis ran up the stairs to answer my father's distress call and see what was hap-pening. He ran past me—I don't think he saw me at all. A mo-ment later, Dennis came back, presumably to grab the gun. My father began to lose his grip on the younger man and before he could regain his composure, I witnessed the man with the axe swinging wildly, bringing the tool down bluntly on my father's back and shoulder.

There was blood everywhere. It seemed to be splattered across every inch of the dingy white asbestos of the basement. A harsh metal scent of the mingled blade and blood that left no surface untouched clouded the air. A thought rang out in my mind that I should run, but I was immobilized with fear and horror, yet still had a strange desire to see what was going to happen next. I thought Dennis had the sense to run and remembered him dashing past me, his eyes focused, but now he had come back.

When Dennis went past me, I heard his sniffles and could see him shaking. He was, after all, only seven years old at the time. Then I could clearly see why; he raised his hand, slowly at first, and then in a sudden cataclysm of action, he displayed the gun he had been carrying. Without warning, one of the men plowed into young Dennis and threw him across the cellar floor. He had wrestled the gun free from his small hands. Suddenly, during the struggle, the gun went off—the two shots, each horrifying and distinct as the sound of the bullets clanged off the basement walls.

I saw my father's eyes widen, as did the other men's. They were all expecting to die, I could see it on their faces. They all had a moment where they were waiting to look down and see a fatal wound bleeding, sending them to their deaths, but none of them dropped.

Springing to action first, my father took advantage of the stunned, awful silence and pounced his enemy, wresting the gun from him, wailing on him, beating his face, neck and body as he went. I am quite certain that if the police hadn't arrived at that moment, he would have beat the man to death.

The police invaded the bloody scene, handcuffing the men roughly with little concern for their injuries. Dennis shakily, but with a newfound look of bravery on his face, limped up the stairs past me, tracking my mother and father's blood as he went. I remember sitting there for a long time. Letting it sink in, even if I didn't want to think about it.

I was four years old at the time I watched all of this happen.

And this is my first memory.

Looking All the Way Back...

I wish I could find a way to rattle off a host of pristine, fond memories of my youth-of my time growing up in a nice, quaint town in Rhode Island. I would like to be able to share some kind of deeply personal memories of joy, laughter— something that would allow me to be sentimental. I want to create in my memory the sense that there might have been days spent lost in play and imagination with my siblings, but this would be a sheer creation and fabrication of something that did not happen and this book is about the truth. The truths are harsh, my stomach recoils as I relate them.

I wish I could tell you things that wouldn't make you cringe to hear. But I think we both know that it is not the case, that my story is not going to make you smile or laugh delightedly. There is nothing innocent, nothing free from the stains of growing up in the Burt family.

I so badly want to tell you that my memories—even the bad ones—have been glossed over with the forgetful magic of time. That they have, over the space of long years, somehow diminished in their terrific horror. But this is not something I can say either because if anything, the gravity of what I know, have seen, and have lived through have made the opposite true. Each day new, keen and awful realizations overwhelm me. I often sit stunned in the face of what has been and what continues to exist in the wake of Frances Burt. Frances Burt and her family. A family that I am, regrettably, inevitably, a part of despite the lack of contact I've kept with them over many years. I cannot sleep. Nothing helps. The curse of my bloodline drags me along, and despite my resistance, ushers me down painful paths during the many long, vacant nights.

I tell myself they are gone now, that they don't matter. But they will always matter because we are, inevitably and sadly for me anyway, the whole sum of our experiences. Even if they are out of my life they are not out of my mind, not for one sick minute. And then, just as I find myself growing comfortable in a moment of joy or wholeness, something will happen to jerk me back to reality. *You are never free* says this small, persistent voice.

And nothing quiets it.

But my ties with the Burts are severed. I helped put them out of commission for a while. I am hated—despised by all of them. Abhorred by my own flesh and blood and worse still, hated too by people I meet or become acquainted with because of the cumbersome legacy of the Burt family name. People always find out where I come from, who my "people" are. And from that moment on, I am an automatic criminal. Even if before they saw my true heart—saw my softness, sensitivity, tenderness—the moment they learn my name, their eyes shade over. I am not trusted. I want to scream to the world that I am not a Burt, that a name is only a name, but the world too often thinks in generalities, especially when the extent of criminal pasts are involved.

I have not spoken to my family in so many years that it no longer matters—I am dead to them, they are dead to me. At least this is what I say, what I want to believe.

Don't get me wrong, it's not just that I have ceased to have contact and it's my own efforts alone that are preventing contact. After helping law enforcement bring a grand end to the decades of gross criminal activity, it's probably quite imaginable that they wouldn't exactly welcome me home with open arms. They do, after all, hate me. But then again, what meaning is there in being hated by some of the most hated people who ever lived on the East Coast of this great country, right?

So yes, all things considered, I wish I could go back in time and run away, stop it all somehow, turn back the clock and fix things—make them somehow normal or right. But in the Burt family with the matriarch, my mother, at the helm, nothing could ever possibly be normal. Not by any means. If I had succeeded in running away or breaking free from the family (and others did, sometimes several times) I would have been brought back. Things would have been worse than before.

It was a cage and oddly, it's one I still feel like I am living in to this day. The bars are no longer visible to the naked eye of an outsider, but I am still locked inside.

The cage is something I hate but it's something that over the years I've become so accustomed to being inside that I don't always notice its steely cold bars. I can see the outside world but I can never touch it full-on with my hands. I am here but I am not.

This is how I felt as a child, this is how I feel now. And my childhood memories carry the stain, the weight, the enormous sensation of isolation—even when surrounded by so many people. A weight that is so cumbersome it makes me feel underwater some days. Nothing was pure then, nor is it now because of my parents—my mother—and this includes my childhood. The same holds true for any of the childhoods of any of the children who ever had the misfortune of becoming subjects of Empress Frances and her maniacal whims.

Because like so many things in the Burt family, nothing can be left untouched or be allowed to remain pure, whole, true, and meaningful. A child and his memories could only be something good if they could be used to manipulate or gain something, and memories seldom have such significance.

To be fair, to provide structure as I muddle through this thick sludge of memory, I will start at the beginning—where I first begin to know what it is to remember.

Forgetting would be difficult. What I remember is much more brutal, more powerful and intense than any ordinary childhood event that is supposed to cling in the memory of an average American child—a child raised according to the standard, the ideal, the dream.

But there was nothing ideal about growing up in the Burt family. And any dreams quickly became nightmares.

*   *   *   *   *

Reversing Memory

My childhood, at least as I remember it, is best described in visceral phrases; splashes of blood, agonized screams of pain, murderous rage. I could not have summoned those words in youth but would have known their meaning instinctively and defined them as describing my first recollections perfectly.

My first memory is a bloody memory—one that was recounted previously and one that is savage in its intensity and makes me cringe to see it played out, especially since I still see it through the eyes of a four year-old child. I am still that child in some ways—scared, confused, but most of all, horrified by what I saw and what I continue to see in my memory.

But in retrospect, what is just as horrifying now is that I grasp not just the fact that I witnessed what I did as a child, but more importantly, the reason behind the violence, and I am even more appalled. This was not a bloody battle to settle some deep feud between men. It wasn't even erupting from a legitimate argument over something concrete that warranted a clash of opinions strong enough to necessitate violence. This event simply stemmed from my father's brazen effort to get tenants removed from the building—rent paying tenants, but ones who hassled him about fixing and maintaining things he should have been doing as a landlord. And ones who were taking up an apartment that my father suddenly decided he wanted for his friend and girlfriend to move into.

You see, in the Burt family, the way of doing business, especially as far as tenants were concerned, there was no such thing as using the proper legal channels to bring about an eviction. If the Burts wanted you out; you'd better believe, you were going to get the hell out. And fast. Or else.

If you dared complain about roaches or asked for an ounce more than my parents thought you were entitled to, you were as good as gone. It wouldn't matter that you paid your rent; lots of people do so and do it regularly. It wouldn't matter if you were quiet and kept your space tidy. Lots of people did the same thing. What mattered was whether or not they liked you, which also often meant whether or not you just kept your mouth shut and went along with anything and everything they might tell you to do or say. In other words, raise a fuss, call attention to yourself as a tenant in any way, and you would be putting yourself in some danger. Real danger.

A BEAUTIFUL DAY IN THE NEIGHBORHOOD

The fight that comprised my first memory was over an apartment that my father wanted cleared out to make room for his friend, Fred, and his girlfriend. Not that my father was the type to have a lot of friends. To my family, friends were useless unless they could be manipulated easily or had some other way to add value or personal gain, but Dad did like Fred. It was always sort of strange to me, even though I didn't think much of it then, but Fred was a bit younger than my father and even though he wasn't close in age to my brothers, they still took a liking to the man. Dad seemed a lot more interested in Fred than in any of us, at least interested in a different way.

Fred was the sort of guy my dad could hang out with, maybe only to feel young again. I think another reason he liked Fred was because they were a lot alike, age differences aside. The one thing they had in common was a complete lack of remorse or willingness to do anything by the book. Case in point; they would go off fishing together, just like a couple of "normal" guys might do on a lazy summer Sunday. But in true Burt fashion, even this couldn't be free from a criminal element. You see, instead of going out in nature they would secretly park just near the private property of a fish hatchery, cut a hole in the fence, raid the fully-stocked ponds with giant nets, and bring home entire coolers full of fresh-caught fish. That's the kind of fun my father liked to have, and this is who he liked to go do things with—someone who also took pleasure in bending the law.

Another thing about Fred; he liked his beer. I barely remember a time when he wasn't drunk. Hand in hand with this fact is that he also liked to beat the hell out of his poor girlfriend, Jane. You see, Fred wasn't what you'd call a happy drunk, dancing around and proclaiming deep love for everyone and falling over himself. Not at all. Fred was one of those Dr. Jekyll and Mr. Hyde drunks. Once he started drinking, and with the more alcohol he put away, the meaner he would become. In no time that lighthearted frizzy-haired character of a kid who had become a permanent fixture in our lives during that time turned into a complete beast, someone almost unrecognizable.

Even after all I've been through, I've never understood why some people put up with the things they do—that is a question that's always haunted me, especially after seeing the way my mother used to treat people, only to have them crawling back for more once they'd licked their wounds. But Fred's girlfriend, she really put up with some terrible abuse. I remember Fred's cruelty towards her; how he used to hold her down on the bed and fart on her face, how he used to smack her around, throw her about like a limp doll. When he wasn't drinking, which wasn't often, the two got along fine, but the moment he started getting loaded, it would be anyone's guess how long it would be before Jane limped out of the building with a black eye and bruises.

One night, not too long after Fred had been installed in the apartment that used to belong to the man who got into the axe fight with my dad, my father had to throw Fred out after he beat Jane. My dad knew he could have easily killed her; it was a miracle he hadn't already, but Dad didn't want that kind of mess on his hands as the owner of the building. He never seemed to mind it when Fred beat Jane, but it would just be a big hassle to have the cops out investigating a homicide at his property, not to mention the mess it would have caused. After all, Fred and Jane were interesting to both of my parents, they wanted to keep them healthy because they had potential; Jane because she had the ability to be used for whatever money she had coming in, as well as the potential for another baby that my parents could use for money, and my father had an interest in her because, inevitably, he wanted to have sex with her. At the time, we all knew Fred would be allowed back, but we didn't expect to see him as soon as we did.

Who knows what Fred did for the first part of the night dad kicked him off the property, but it didn't take him long to come storming back in a drunk fury. At about 2 a.m. I awoke to terrified screams. A weak and bruised Jane was outside, furiously banging on the door, tearfully, desperately calling out for help. Recognizing whose screaming it was, my dad immediately dashed outside. No one needed to tell him what was going on. He instinctively knew that an even drunker Fred had come back to the place and was intent on finishing what he started.

I wasn't fully awake but I remember hurrying down the stairs after my father, expecting to find Fred out front or chasing after Jane, but to my surprise, like a brutal ape, he was shimmying up the columns that led to the third floor apartment from where Jane had fled. He had a long butcher knife between his teeth. This fact, along with his mad drunken effort to climb up the column, made him look like he had a crazy smile on his face—for all I knew, he was smiling with the thought of what he was about to do. My father went after him and just as he was about to get him the police arrived, sirens blaring, lights flashing. They knew that when a call came out to them from the Burt's property, they were going to encounter something violent.

I know that if Jane hadn't screamed and if someone hadn't called the police Fred would have finally killed her. Yes, he might have been sorry about it once he dried out in prison, but the look in his eyes that night communicated no understanding for what he was going to do. No compassion, no feeling, only blind rage—a certain chilling sort of blankness. That's the kind of scary individual Fred was. Looking back, sometimes I think it was that simple wildness and unpredictability that my dad liked, he could make him do anything he wanted, however he wanted, and Fred would do it without remorse. However, this is one of the reasons why he should have kept Fred alone and separated from everyone else.

Fred was a part of our lives for a good long time between his stints in jail, which were numerous. He eventually got locked up and decided he'd had enough of the cycle and hung himself in his cell. However, none of us believed that it truly was a "suicide," instead believing that he had been killed by either a fellow prisoner or a prison guard. Conveniently, the cameras had gone off in his cell the night he died.

I know that Fred and my dad, if they were ever forced to confess, very likely did some things that would make me shudder to learn about—even after all I know already. Like my dad, Fred thrived on the thrill of doing something that would cause harm; he loved the sheer rush that came with destroying something. I think that was why he liked fire, liked the idea of burning down a building, so much. It was the control factor. It was the rush. The idea of destroying something so completely in matter of mere moments tickled his sickness and this arsonist's streak in his personality and made him very useful for my parents, especially when what they needed most was to get rid of a building, which happened often and provided the family with tremendous wealth from the sky-high insurance claims.

They really liked it when Fred, with his lust to burn and destroy, left the cottage at our new, big house on Spring Street a charred skeleton of what it was. For my parents, having someone around who would jump at the chance to do the dirty work was a blessing—the very best kind of friend to have and one of the most valuable.

And yes, that cottage burned; there wasn't much left after

that day I watched from an upper-story window as a screaming drunk Fred let his wildness out, throwing Molotov cocktails through the windows. Oftentimes, he would miss completely but he did a good enough job that my mother got what she wanted.

You see, my mother really, really wanted that house on Spring Street. However, there was an obstacle—and Frances Burt was not one to respond favorably or appropriately to anything that might stand in the way of what she saw as rightfully hers. The owners of the property had been unwilling to come down on the price because they saw value in the cottage and wanted it to be included with the property. In fact, they had written up two separate contracts on the property, but mother had wanted it all included in one contract. The sellers refused to do this. Finally, they came to individual prices on both buildings, and Mother ended up signing the contract. Then, the owners of the house went back on their word after the contract was signed and decided to up the price on the cottage, which really made my mother mad. The whole situation was a nuisance for my mother, especially since someone was daring to go against her wishes and defy her demands. This is when she got the idea that if the cottage was destroyed, there is no way the owners of the property could charge her what they wanted to charge. That's when Fred set it on fire. As you can imagine then, with the precious cottage in burnt ruins (for the most part it was still salvageable enough after some renovations to move her friends into) my mother was pleased.

For the first time, my mother was really growing to understand what a great thing arson was. A devastating fire produced riches far faster than anything else—and with such minimal risk! This knowledge sparked a revolution in her understanding of how to really get what she desired and left Fred satisfied, at least for a time, since he was able to see his rage blaze before his eyes.

Even as I sat there watching it burn, listening to the

drunken ramblings of my father's good friend Fred, I remember liking the cottage; it got my imagination going. At one time, it probably served as servant's quarters and I imagine, especially as an adult who today understands the significance and worth of the building, like the main house itself, had a great deal of local historical significance. Then again, that wouldn't have meant a damn thing to anyone in my family, but looking back I remember how grand the place seemed with its regal grounds and multitude of buildings that once served to house a family of local upper-class citizens. For my mother, it looked like something upper-class and that was all that mattered because after all, her aim in life was to have everything presented in as high-class of a style as possible—and to do so no matter what the cost was or what she had to do to attain that lifestyle.

I knew she told Fred to go ahead and do it knowing he'd have no complaints about the task. That's all something I'll get to in a moment. The house on Spring Street became the center of our lives for a long, long time but the cottage incident, which kicked off not one fire but countless others my family was involved in, marked the beginning of an era for the Burt family.

Saints and Royalty

Our town was one of extremes in terms of class; from the endless streets of nearly identical run-down tenement houses, several of which my family owned and "took care of" (meaning they collected rent and that's the end of it) to the high-end homes like the one we moved into on Spring Street; social class was never hard to determine. In Pawtucket, you were either rich or you were poor, period. And my mother made damn sure we weren't ever perceived as poor—that would, after all, be a crime in her eyes.

Pawtucket's history is closely associated with the textile industry in New England, which was a major aspect of the town's history from the time of the industrial revolution onward. I imagine our huge place there on Spring Street once housed a local textile factory owner or rich merchants. It seems silly to me to think in these terms since my family only saw the place as a big house in a desirable area, but I see now what an atrocity it was that our family single-handedly ruined the place. That's just the way my parents were though; nothing had any value if there wasn't an immediate way to assign an attainable dollar value to it and then promptly collect.

So much of what happened in Pawtucket revolved around social class; the lawyers, the insurance, city officials and agency leaders, the police—everyone had their allegiances, their protected friends. So many of these alliances weren't based on what you would typically want in a community either; it was based on who had more money than who and who would be the most willing to pay up to get what was desired. My mom in particular had a knack for getting exactly what she wanted from any number of Pawtucket's finest citizens and, by the time we moved into our stately house on Spring Street and out of our old system of owner-occupied (that would be us as the owners) tenement living, my mother had a neat knack for pocketing people who mattered and I believe this was through a combination of cash "donations" and conversations I overheard.

Looking back, we were Pawtucket royalty. But this wasn't a kind of friendly or benevolent sort of rule; it was a dictatorship and Frances Burt, my mother, was that dictator. Based on my own observations it seemed as if she had everyone in her pocket and no one who knew better would ever dare defy her—including any of her children, her husband, and of course, children's services agencies, insurance representatives, and lawyers.

My mother was literally obsessed with appearances. With wealth, and it's creation, at all costs, be it the costs, material, or otherwise, and with the illusion of perfection. However, the things that were going on in our lives, from the time we were born until we were finally old enough to realize how drastically abnormal what we experienced was, were anything but perfect. What we, all of the children who ever lived under the rule of Frances Burt, knew was that the veneer of perfection masked realties that were so grim, so horrible, that they would live on in the dreadful tales that will likely be told about our family for years to come.

The tales you might have heard are probably true. I put nothing past any member of my family. I continually learn about the ghastly nature and extent of their crimes and am never surprised when something new emerges.

Because Frances Burt, my mother, was the embodiment of evil. She raised us to be demons, to be tricksters, criminals spawned by hellfire.

Does that sound like an overstatement? Do you believe that someone can exist with that goal? Without the innate capability of looking at another person as a human being and not simply a flesh and blood source of financial gain? My mother had no empathy. No concern for suffering. No sense of right, of wrong, of good, and I wonder sometimes if she had no sense of wrongdoing either. It all seemed so clear-cut for her—by simply eliminating any attempt at asking herself moral questions, she was able to live quite happily in the depths of ultimate depravity. Because she never thought about it, I really do not think she ever allowed herself to feel remorse. Because after all, what financial gain could anyone possibly extract from moral questions? Pity and empathy were for suckers, for idiots.

If you had any idea—and I will try my hardest to give you a sense of this—of what happened in our family, you would be left with no other claim to make about her. She felt nothing, cared for no one, and saw nothing emotional or genuine as worthwhile unless there was a price, a concrete dollar amount associated with it.

This was especially true with children; after all, given the ridiculously "generous" benefits of adopting children, who wouldn't want to have a house full of kids?

Yes, of course, she already had her own children, but they were really of little value and were always doing something to infuriate her—like wetting the bed or not properly playing along with her tricks to get money out of anyone she could. Foster kids? Now that's another story—they had some real potential. How great could it be for my mother to be paid by the state for slaves? It was too good to be true for her; here she was, being handed money to keep these children and do whatever she wanted with them. These children ended up making her more money than any of her natural children could have and saved her a bundle in housekeeping and employees to keep up with the work that needed to be done on the apartments.

Little goldmines, those children.

To Be a Child....

Childhood was not sacred to my mother. Nothing was. Everything about her might have seemed, to the distant viewer, to be normal—to be exactly what you'd expect of a typical upper class mother and wife, but on the underside of things was a dark, nasty reality.

What is most shocking to me is that my mother, who was one of the most brutal women—or people—I have ever known, was allowed to have so many children under her care. I am mystified, horrified, appalled. Because out of all women who should have been banned from even being around children, let alone raising them, my mother was given all of them she wanted—and some she didn't want but knew would be useful to her down the road.

If nothing else, my story serves as a grim reminder of some of the worst failings of a children's welfare system. A system that overlooked countless signs and warnings. A system that saw what it wanted to see in Frances Burt. And yes, my mom was a superior actress and yes, we could clearly afford to take on more kids. But God, the level of oversight is astounding.

When those children, first Marie, Ricky, L.J., and poor LeeAnn, came to our home, I knew what they were in for. And when the others followed along after that, I knew that they were in for it too. The beatings, the verbal abuse, the sexual abuse at the hands of my father—if I'm thankful for anything it's that I never had the misfortune of being a girl.

And while I wasn't a girl and subjected to the sick kinds of things Marie, LeeAnn, Rachel, and others had to put up with for years on end, I had my own bit of misfortune. You see, I was a bed-wetter. And Frances Burt did not like little bed-wetters. Not at all.

One thought, one nostalgic sidelong glance at something that reminds me of those days—one shot of scent that whips me back to my youth and I am there again. I am always reliving what I have tried for so many years to forget… I cannot help but fall into the memory, live again and see through the eyes of a child.

It is some ridiculous hour. All of the others are asleep. The smell of urine drenched pajama shorts and the stale air of the closet is nauseating. I sit with my knees pulled tight to my chest. I don't dare move and rustle anything on the closet floor. I mustn't make a sound. If I stay perfectly still maybe she will pass by my room and look for me elsewhere. I hear her footsteps off in the distance and the sound of the morning routine beginning. My heart pounds so loudly that it seems to echo and reverberate throughout the closet. I pull my knees closer to my chest in hopes of muffling the thud of my heart. The closet is dark, and I am terrified of the blackness, but it is better than facing her.

I hadn't intended on staying here all night. Even though I had willed myself to stay awake – I had failed. My plan was to sleep in the closet until daybreak, change my pajamas, move back to my bed and she would find me there sleeping. I had figured out how to escape the inevitable – or so I thought. It didn't happen like that. I fell asleep and daybreak passed while I was still in the closet. And now, she is coming.

I don't have enough time. Her footsteps are closer and I hear my heart about to give me away. She is in my room, calling my name, and she is irritated. The closet door swings open and the light from the day rushes over me. I squint and can barley make out the figure standing in the doorway of the closet – but I know it is her. Before my eyes can adjust to the light, I see her hands move towards me and I instinctively cover my head with both arms. In one motion, she grabs me and has a hold of me. With her one hand wrapped around my wrists she yanks me to my feet. I am yanked screaming from the closet and she drags me into the kitchen. She is more angry than normal; she is furious that I tried to fool her.

Her hand still firmly around both of my wrists, she uses her free hand to jerk open the wooden drawer and extract her weapon. It is always her weapon of choice and she is a masterful operator. She adjusts it in her hand with expert proficiency. She grasps the end with the plug and the other end with the sockets and makes a loop. The extension cord is ready. She swings hard and swoops the cord down towards my legs. I intuitively jump to one side to miss the whip, but as usual, I fail. It catches me on the calf and the pain jolts through my body.

She pulls me closer and swings a second time, this time connecting on my side. I twist and move as the third strike comes. This time, she misses the full contact intended and only catches me on the upper thigh. She readjusts her grip on my wrists and pulls me closer. She is frustrated that I maneuvered away and didn't get the full impact of her swing. She pulls the cord back over her head, her annoyance gives her new purpose and she makes contact with my thighs. I squat and try to fall the ground, but her grip is too tight. She holds me while I dangle and she swings the cord again and again, making a connection each time on my thighs, my ribs, my back and my stomach. I can feel my flesh welting and my skin breaking open. She shoves me backwards and raises the cord above her head like a lasso and plunges the cord toward me, it snaps against my legs. She's in rhythm now, she reaches out and grabs one of my arms. I pull hard and drop to the floor on my back. My signature move. Lying on the floor in the kitchen, I hold my feet and legs straight up in the air and she circles me now, trying to get an open shot of my body. I move with her – scrambling on my back, sliding on the floor — trying to defend myself. She lifts and lowers the cord several more times as I shuffle to shield myself. Without warning, she turns, places the cord in the drawer and pulls me to my feet. The dance is over. My skin is raw and some of the welts are bleeding. The urine, on pajama shorts, it is rubbing against some of my wounds – stinging them. She thrusts me towards the bathroom, instructing me to go clean myself up and get ready for school. The audience at the kitchen table applauds and cheers. The morning entertainment had not disappointed.

I am five years old, and I have survived another "whip dance" with my mother.

Tonight, I promise myself, I will not wet the bed. I cannot. I must not. But I always do and I am so angry that I would lash myself some nights if I could.

It was the most gut-wrenching sense of helplessness I have ever known. Being out of control of my own body at night, not realizing when I had to get up and pee was bad enough. I was humiliated by it for my own sake. The worst part though, was that it was the one thing that my mom could not stand. It drove her completely out of her skull when I would do it.

But goddamn, no matter what-I just couldn't help it. It was not anything I could control. It was that plain and simple; I was powerless.

I used to try to stay awake all night; struggling to keep my eyes open through the endless nights in my cold room, praying to be alert, praying because I knew that if I let my eyes slide closed, even for a moment, I would tumble into the dark world of sleep and no matter what I tried to do about it, no matter what denials I tried to arrange in my head at nightfall, I would not have control during sleep and would wet my clothes.

I tried everything. I even tried to lay at the end of the bed sideways so that if I did pee I could get up, change clothes, jump up and if she pulled the sheet back she wouldn't see it. I also tried to fall asleep in the closet any night I thought I could get away with it but that never worked either. She would always find me there, afraid, shaking, humiliated at the pee on the floor of my closet.

She would come in before dawn, it seemed that she almost hoped she would find me there—almost like she felt the urge to beat the living hell out of someone but needed a reason in the middle of the night. She'd tear open the closet door, get a death-grip on my wrists and drag me into the kitchen for a beating.

The worst thing was the electrical cord. Being slapped around, kicked, even punched I could deal with, but the electrical cord was the one thing that sent me to my knees. The thought, even all these years later, makes me feel weak, tired, and like a frightened child. The electrical cord was serious business; there was even a grim sort of formal procedure that was followed when it was called upon, which for a long time during my youth, was each and every day.

You see, there was this drawer, and all it contained was electrical cords, it was the sole purpose, the only use for this drawer. Inside there were several, all of them alike in their snaky, sharp coils and all roughly equivalent in the amount of flesh they could wick away. And while it might seem like it would be a little "easier" to have a nice thin little whip of an electrical cord versus one of the heavy-duty, double-thickness insulated ones, let me tell you, that is not at all the case. The thin ones gathered a horrible, instant horsewhip-like quality with one swift action of a practiced wrist (and her wrist knew instinctively which angles would make us scream) and cracked into the skin clean as a whistle and sharp as a razor.

And here's the really nasty thing about those electrical cords and the system behind those beatings, there were times when she would take her level of sadism to a new level. It was during these times where she would not reach for them. That would make it too easy, too much like a normal beating, not give enough time for us to think about the horror and pain and sting that waited. No. The worst kind of beating would be when I would have to go up to the drawer, approach it like some kind of awful sleeping demon, open it, and select a cord. I would, therefore, end up bringing the punishment on myself, seeming to invite it in despite the fact it was never welcome—only grimly anticipated.

There is no pain like that pain. There is no way to relate this kind of pain to anyone who has never had a lashing with something so thin and firm that it slices rather than smacks or strikes.

This was my life for many years. Night after night, afraid to sleep, dawn after endless dawn, shameful to have fallen asleep, to be brutally beaten for the one thing that I was completely powerless over despite all efforts.

To her, I was lazy and stupid—too unmotivated and dumb to know that I had to pee. In my heart I knew better, but none of that meant anything. I just couldn't stay awake and school was miserable as I sat there at my hard-seated desk, unable to keep from nodding off, only able to stay awake because of the burning pain caused by the bright bloody red welts that went across my back and legs. Just sitting there at my desk would reopen the wounds that would be freshly laid almost on a daily basis; I remember that sickening sensation that was all too familiar during my youth—the feeling of blood making my pants stick to my skin.

It hurt to walk, it hurt to sit.

It hurt to be alive then.

Family Films

I tried to think back to the times I might have done something with my family—experienced something wholesome, untainted by the constant gravitation toward something wrong. I tried, but everything that might have started out as something a "normal" family might do ended badly. It was almost as if my parents were playing some sort of sick joke on us, whether they meant to or not. I actually don't think they thought much about it in those terms. As kids we were just fulfilling our functions as distracters or accessories to crimes we weren't fully aware of.

For some reason, one of the darkest themes from my childhood is something that other kids would consider, looking back, as some of the best times with their family and friends — an outing to the movies. It wasn't planned this way or anything but I'll tell you, it seemed like anytime my parents were involved with a theater, something bad was going to go down.

I remember, for instance, when, for the first time and the only time, my father took me to the movies.

I was so thrilled to have a day out of the house; a whole afternoon with my father—just the two of us, going to a matinee like a good, normal father and son would do. He had chosen me especially to go with him and this realization filled me with such a great sensation that I will never forget it. Out of all of my other brothers, he picked me, and boy, was I ever excited. I remember that I'd just been on the receiving end of a particularly bad beating and while I was sore and knew that the ride there in the car would reopen my back and leg wounds, I jumped at the chance for an outing with my dad.

As we got in our car, I remembering feeling like all was right with the world. To my delight, my dad pulled into the big parking lot at the Four Seasons Cinema. My father bought our tickets, put his arm on my shoulder as we entered and for the first time in my life until that point I got the distinct sense that this was how things were supposed to be. Everything was right. We laughed our asses off at the showing of *Blazing Saddles* and had a wonderful time. Nothing could touch me that afternoon—I remember that the injuries from my beating that morning had taken a backseat, I didn't feel them at all.

As we walked out of the movie, laughing, I noticed that my dad suddenly became serious—his laughter and good cheer with me ended as soon as we were out of sight and then, before I knew anything, things were back to like they always had been—like I wasn't even really there with him any longer. He looked nervous for a moment and a strange spark lit his eyes as he scanned the parking lot.

"The car is gone, someone stole it. I gotta call the police now," he said out loud, not sounding surprised in the least—like he knew full well before even looking in the lot that the car would be gone.

I stared blankly at him, "Dad, it's right over there—look," and I pointed but it wasn't ours.

He looked at me for a moment like I was stupid. "It's gone. You got that?" he said, shaking his head. Instead of looking for it at all, he made his way to the payphone, where he called my mother.

I didn't catch all of the conversation, but I heard enough to know that Dad had forgotten and left the keys in the car. Since the car was "stolen" by Jude, Dad knew that there was a possibility that the reporting cop on the scene would ask for the keys and it would look suspicious if he didn't have them. He was calling my mother to see if she could get up there before the police did with an extra key, to make the story look plausible.

The cops arrived, took the description and information and during that endless hour, our car—that car I fully expected to ride back in with my father while we talked and laughed about the movie we went to see—was being driven to another state where it would be torched beyond recognition.

It was found of course, charred and burned in Seekonk,

Massachusetts and made my parents one hell of a lot of money in an insurance claim.

It was clear enough I'd been used as a sort of decoy—as an aid to help my dad look like the kind of stand-up man who did things like drop everything to go have some quality time with his son for an afternoon. Yeah, we enjoyed ourselves and I'll never forget laughing our asses off there in that theater, but it's completely tarnished by my realization later that the whole time he was probably just running over in his mind how things were going to go down when we finally got out of there. It really ruins it as a bonding experience, but why would I ever think that bonding would be anything he'd have an interest in anyway? My parents just weren't that sort of people, to say the least.

With the Four Seasons fiasco in mind, I can rationalize it all away by saying that Dad wanted money for a new car and I happened to be along for the ride. There was a method to the madness—an ultimate goal behind something that ended up making me feel pretty shitty when all was said and done. But the night my mom and dad loaded a bunch of us kids up in the station wagon to go to a drive-in (and boy, weren't we excited then too) really takes the cake. Because that night, the cruelty didn't really have a function or an end goal of gain in sight—it was just plain cruel.

Our first drive-in experience happened well before my little outing with dad at the Four Seasons; I think I was probably six or so. We were packed like sardines into the car that night—my brothers, along with Candace and I goofed around the whole ride, we were so damn excited. Bruce was just born and mom brought him along, screaming and fussing at all the commotion in the tight space of the car. We had a rough idea of what a drive-in movie was, we'd all seen the theaters outside with their big blank white screens reflecting the afternoon sun, but we were like big kids now—out at night, doing something only older kids and adults did. It was awesome.

There were two different screens in separated lots at this

drive-in and cars were packed in for both. I knew that one of the new monster movies was playing and I felt like the coolest kid in the world when I realized that Godzilla Versus Megalon was playing at the drive-in. "What have we done to deserve a treat like this?" I thought to myself, bouncing excitedly in my seat. We couldn't wait for the film to begin. The experience itself was unlike anything we'd known—the darkness of night sets in and my parents positioned the speakers to allow sound from the movie into the car.

The movie began with a slow start, not much appears to be happening. There is a girl they keep showing, she's probably ten or so—a little older than me—and there are a lot of adults. I wait and wait but still no Godzilla. Still no Megalon. Growing antsy, I crane my neck to see what's going on at the other movie screen. From a distance, over the impatient head of Candace, I can see Godzilla storming around, preparing for battle. "There's been some mistake," I think to myself—"we're at the wrong movie." Clearly my parents must know, I was sure of it. I spoke up to tell them that this isn't Godzilla versus Megalon but my mom told me to shut up. She is engrossed in what is on the screen, as is my father. Their eyes are wide and expectant, just like the eyes of the kids who were watching Godzilla on the other screen—the kids I wanted to be like. I was frustrated, but I suppose I was still glad to be out and about watching a drive-in movie with the older kids. I snuck furtive glances at the cars around us. The silhouettes of the people in those cars didn't look like those of children; it was all adults, people in pairs sitting stiff and upright, a certain tension about their postures as they watched.

I made myself pay attention to the movie that my parents are so wrapped up in. Candace joined me and we both became quiet. The boring adults talking to the peppy little girl soon gives way to something far more horrifying that I could have ever expected or imagined to be possible. Without warning, this little girl has turned ugly—very ugly, and scary. She is evil; her head spins around 360 degrees and she says things like "fuck me" to a priest that seems to want to help her. She stabs herself and blood pours out of her, she vomits and spews words that I could not then completely understand but knew I wasn't supposed to say. She took a cross and began stabbing herself with that too and at that point, with the sick cackle of my parents' laughter and glee in the background, I covered my ears. I focused all of my attention on the screen across the way—the screen showing the movie I wanted to see. The movie that I was supposed to see, because even then I knew that this was not a movie kids were supposed to see.

Out of all of the things that happened to me growing up, this really was one of the most terrifying and damaging in the long-term things that occurred. I will never forget it, I remember it vividly. I can remember the sound of flesh ripping, the inhuman sounds that came through the speaker. It is seared into my memory and the pain of it might as well have been brandished with a hot iron into the very flesh that surrounds my skull. It was awful. Four-year-old Candace was lucky enough to have lost interest during the adults talking portion of the movie and fell asleep and Bruce was blessed to be a baby with no awareness. I, however, sat frozen in my utter terror, unable to leave or move or do anything but make myself blank and see only what I wanted until it was all over.

I would have gladly taken that awful, dreaded, nubby electrical cord to my face, back, legs—wherever she wanted to strike with it—if it could replace that goddamned film. I wonder if any adults present at that drive-in looked over at our car and saw our wholesome-looking little family watching *The Exorcist* and wondered what kind of parents would let their kindergartners watch as a girl, not much older, bloodied herself with a cross and said things that even the most vile teenager might have a difficult time mustering. This was one of the most traumatic moments of my childhood and it has stuck with me my entire life. To this day, it is impossible for me to watch that film without begin transported back to that night, as a six-year old, sitting in the back of my parent's station wagon, being terrified out of my wits, while my parents laughed happily in the front seats of the car.

It is these same parents who were allowed to foster one child after another. If that is not a lapse in the "welfare" part of child welfare, then I don't what is.

I don't know if it was because of that damned film or because of my own imagination, but I remember around that time that I was just scared to hell at the very thought of the devil — of demons. This idea disturbed me beyond any other. And the problem was I spent so many nights forcing myself to stay awake, nights that I was so tired that even the craziest imaginations started to take on frightening shapes of reality.

When we moved to that giant hulk of a house on Spring Street, which was really an old mansion, complete with creaking floors and more strange, unexplained noises than I ever cared to enumerate, things got even worse. Nights sitting there, hunched up in the bed in fear of my own need to pee versus my need to sleep with nothing to do or think about outside of those odd sounds and senses that the house itself was evil. I was scared to walk down the hallway at night because of that movie, but at the same time I feared the beating I would get in the morning if I couldn't make it to the bathroom in time. Those were some of the worst times of my life; I would be frightened half to death — afraid to sleep in case I had to pee, afraid to move in case I would alert the demons that I was there, afraid for the morning to come just as much as I was afraid of the nighttime itself.

During those days, sore and tired and mentally exhausted, I would walk to school each morning, often with the tender sting of a fresh lash aching or seeping. I would always pass by this massive impressive church, St. Joseph's. I loved to look at it when I passed and one day I gathered up the nerve and went inside. It was quiet, peaceful, safe. No one bothered me and I didn't bother or have to talk to anyone either. It was a special place away from everything and I knew that nothing could touch me there. Nothing could ever come close to me when I had St. Joseph's to protect me, to surround me in its peaceful, stoic, silent embrace. It was a safe haven and it was when I was inside its doors that I allowed my heart to stop racing, my fear to subside. I didn't feel as if I was being pursued when I was at St. Joseph's.

As I grew more comfortable with the idea of St. Joseph's as a special place, I started to go more often. I would get up way early in the morning, way before anyone else, and would steal away. No one ever noticed I was missing. I don't think God was listening to me, but I would beg Him to make the beatings stop. I made Him promises that I would do anything if they would just end, if the misery of my small life would just come to a screeching halt.

But it didn't. Things went on as usual, just as they had before. I still went, sneaking around. It was my secret. I can only imagine what my mom would have said if she knew I'd been going to church. Unlike in the movie, *Family Sins*, my mother had a strong opinion on organized religion. "Church is for worthless idiots" would probably be along the lines of what she'd respond with, to put it mildly. And I would probably get the shit beat out of me for it on top of that.

Later, as more kids entered our family, my relationship with this God and St. Joseph's changed a little as a searing sense of guilt set in. As I got just a little older (and I went to church in secret for a long time during my youth) I did eventually stop wetting the bed. And I don't know if it's just that or if she just had some fresh meat to tear into, but the beatings did begin to slow down in frequency.

About the time I started getting beaten a little less regularly is when several other kids joined our family. She laid into them with that electrical cord. She laid into them with her bare hands. She tore them apart, physically and mentally.

And I felt so damn guilty. The whole time I felt so terrible because in my mind, this was happening to them because God enacted a dark sort of substitution. To replace my pain and suffering, He made others suffer in my place. These kids were having the living hell beaten out of them and I wasn't, and I felt like it was my doing somehow—like I had a part in their greatest source of misery.

This guilt probably also stemmed from a secret longing that really set in when I'd see my mom on the prowl, out for a kill for the day, that she'd lay into someone else. I wanted it to be the others and not me. Yes, that's just a natural sense of self-preservation but that kind of thick, heavy guilt is a lot to live with.

Eventually, my secret visits to St. Joseph's were more spaced out and before long I didn't go at all. If He'd been listening, He got my message all wrong at least in most parts. I knew one thing though, it had provided me a safe haven and it was the only place I had ever felt safe as a child. I have much to thank St. Joseph's for, that I know for sure. One of the saving graces that the institution had sent my way was my wife, Arlean. She is nothing but an angel to me and always has been, but I knew she came my way because I needed an intervention in my life. Maybe God didn't answer all my prayers, but He got it right with her. Arlean helped stop me from taking the path that I was about to walk down and, while my mother always said that Arlean was a bad person and responsible for "corrupting" me, I know different. Arlean was and is my guardian angel, that much I know.

SEEING AND SENSING

The whole idea of something being inappropriate for young minds or young eyes didn't really stick with my parents—either of them. By the time I was a teenager, I could handle looking at just about anything, blood and guts, the aftermath of violence, people crying, begging, and screaming because of something either my mom or dad did to fuck them over, to screw up their lives permanently. I'm not going to say I didn't feel anything ever, it's just that after a while you get so used to certain kinds of things that the full gravity of what it is doesn't strike you until later in life, if ever at all.

I wonder if I got a little bit of that ability to detach from my mom; it might have come from my dad too. Then again, it might just be a result of me being exposed to so much vile shit that over time I formed the ability to detach at will. Some things—a few of which I've already talked a little about—really stuck with me for one reason or another.

One of those strange things that did stay with me over the years and always kind of haunted me (and not just because of what it was but what the reaction was on my mom's part, too) was when my dad's sister—a lady we really didn't really have contact with since mom thought she was trash—lost her son in a car accident. And it was a nasty accident. I know this story because I learned this information from conversations that I listened to between my mother and father.

This cousin of mine, Jake was his name, we didn't know each other really or anything, but I'd heard his name a few times and knew a thing or two about him. We didn't talk to them, by the way, because not only did my mom think that they were trash, but she also pretty much made Dad sever all of his ties with his family, just like she did with anyone else who came into our lives. Anyway, Jake was a drummer in a band—a cool guy, I used to think from my young perspective—and he used to play at bars at night. He had this souped-up Mustang and one night as he was driving home from work with a friend in the car (I always thought that it was probably because he was drunk, because in my opinion he was quite often), he made the decision to go a ridiculous speed down a country road. This was a road that a lot of the younger (to me then, they were much older) kids used to drag race down at all hours of the night. At some point, he lost control of the car, which was topping out at a speed of around 150 mph. In a burst of ballsy quick thinking, as well as an act of salvation, his passenger flat-out bailed—jumping out of the car as it whirled around—and lived to tell about it. Jake, however, wasn't as lucky. The car got cut right in half, the windshield was completely disintegrated, and the motor of the Mustang was in the seats. The cops found his head in one spot, his arms in another, torso in another place—all hundreds of feet apart. It was like he'd been through a deli slicer.

This is some pretty grim knowledge for a little kid of eight or nine to gain on his own; I mean, I suppose it was sobering and a recognition of life and death and all of that, but nothing prepared me for going with my dad out to the junkyard to take a look at what was left of the car. I'm standing there with my dad, who is tearing up as the guy from the scrap yard tells us in graphic detail about where all the body parts were found with a certain sick bit of excitement in his voice and all of a sudden, the guy stopped short and told Dad and I to look at something that had caught his eye. Sitting on part of the mangled heap of metal was a shoe with a sock in it—Jake's, they had to be. On the shoe and inside of the cotton of his old sock was skin. Actual skin, just there, looking like dry skin, like the kind that suddenly bubbles up and begins to peel after a sunburn. On closer inspection, skin was everywhere. The crash had been so powerful that he literally came right out of his shoes and socks so fast that it tore big bunches of his skin off with it. Part of it was because barbed wire slicked through the car as it spun and besides, at 150 miles per hour, that's just what happens—it rips you right out of your skin. Sickening. I could feel my stomach churning.

So I guess what I'm saying is that from a young age, I'd been exposed to some dark stuff. But the real point of this story isn't really about just that. After all, lots of kids are unwittingly witnesses to accidents or see awful things happen before their eyes.

The main part of what was disturbing about this whole affair was the way my mom reacted to this death.

Like I said before, my mom thought most people on my dad's side of the family were trash. She would have been glad if they'd all just gone ahead and died in one big event so she'd never have to bother with recognizing their existence. It's not just that she felt that way, it was that she was so damned cruel in what she said about any of them. They were sub-human. Actually, to my mom, anyone who couldn't be used or manipulated in her eyes was, in one way or another, subhuman. Disposable.

The reason Dad and I had to go to the junkyard to see the car was because my dad felt the need to show his respects somehow or at least recognize the death of his estranged nephew. He really was torn up about the whole thing in a way he seldom ever seemed to be with damn near anything else that happened in our lives. The thing was, after it happened, he said something to mom about going to Jake's funeral. She scoffed immediately at the very idea, "Are you shitting me?" she said, eyes wide. "Those good for nothing people—that's one less of them as far as I'm concerned. The world would be one hell of a lot better place if they'd all do everyone a favor and die. Worthless pieces of shit, all of them."

I remember my dad just looking at her for a moment. It was one of those rare moments when I think he remembered just what kind of heartless monster she was. While I'm not going to say he wasn't pretty heartless and monstrous himself, his heart was not completely empty—there was still enough there to qualify him as human. He told me to come along, which I did since I liked going anywhere as long as it was away from the house and the possibility of getting my ass beat for whatever thing I might do in the meantime, and we drove in silence. He didn't tell me where we were going, he just looked straight ahead and drove, silent.

Things like Jake's accident and the whole event afterwards

stuck in my memory because they reminded me not only of the fact that I saw way more than any eight or nine year-old kid should, but more importantly, that my family was not normal. It was times like this that I knew my mom lacked a soul. I think I knew that before I was eight in some instinctive way, but there was just something so profoundly horrifying at her laughing in reaction to someone else's misery, someone else's death, someone else's loss. It made her happy, those things; misery, death, and loss always did if they happened to someone she didn't care about—and she really didn't care about anyone but herself.

My parents were not worried about what we were exposed to. I sometimes don't even think, in hindsight anyway, that they even thought about certain things not being suitable for our young eyes. When I think about this, I am forced to remember that it wasn't just things she would expose us to, it was images and people.

Frances Burt—the woman who I am so sad to say was my mother—never thought about how things would be perceived from the perspective of childhood. She would proudly show off things, to us and others, that would make a normal person— adult or child—cringe.

She had this picture that she used to show to everyone she "trusted" and especially one she liked to show to her kids. She kept it like a trophy and showed it off as it was a piece of her handiest work—as if it was something to be treasured and held aloft as a symbol of her greatness. I saw this picture many times. I will never forget it—I couldn't if I tried. I wasn't a small kid when I first saw it, but I was young enough that it shook me to core, as it did Marie and all of the other kids who were forced to admire it.

In this prized photograph was a man, although he didn't look like a man at all anymore. He was more of just a torso. His head was shattered and brains lay huddled in gray, bloodied lumps against shag carpet. It was a picture of a man who had been shot at point-blank range with a shotgun in the face. And there was nothing left of anything above the neck that was recognizable as human. Her eyes would glaze over and light up with a strange glow when she looked at that picture. It pleased her. And she wanted others to share in her delight.

In many ways, this was like her shared trophy with my brother Dennis. You see, Dennis was a psychopath—he was Mom's boy all around. Unlike my brother Raymond, who was more like Mom's lapdog, even following her into the bathroom while she did her business to talk to her, to be near his queen, Dennis was straight-up crazy muscle. He was her strong arm when she needed work that only a savage could do and was too dumb to ever try to manipulate her. He was the ideal son in that respect. Anyway, when Dennis was in his late teens I thought he was into dealing drugs big time because he had been convicted on these charges twice and served time in prison on several occasions for other drug charges. There was this time he went with this guy named Tilton Brown to get money for some shit they sold. The guy didn't have the money so they shot out his kneecaps with a shotgun. Scared as hell and eager to do anything to get back at Dennis and Tilton, the guy ratted out the men who crippled him for life.

To make a long story short, not long after all of this started going down, Dennis got pulled over in a car with a backseat covered in blood. They impounded the car, searched missing persons reports—anything to find out how that much blood wound up in Dennis' car. He told the cops he had a nosebleed, which they probably thought was hilarious—they knew only someone getting their brains blown out could have caused a mess like that. Not long after the cops, giving up, released his car did a picture emerge—the same picture that's haunted all of us kids and the one that Mom was so proud of. Dennis told mom he took the picture to prove the guy was dead, had Dad get rid of the gun, and the rest is history.

So no. To my family, there was nothing a kid couldn't see or witness or be exposed to. And there were no people, as long as they were on my mom's side, that we had to avoid either. She never thought once about exposing us to anything—I think she liked seeing us squirm. If nothing else, it reinforced the sense of utter fear for our lives from a young age on down the line.

One thing is for sure, misery loves company. This was the case for my dad (even if love was not something that factored into their strange relationship) and it was certainly the case for my mom. Although now that I think about it, I am not sure if my mom was really ever all that miserable. She was actually what I think some people might call a rather self-satisfied person. She had money and endless sources for making more and for her, I really do think that was enough. What was so strange about her, among thousands of other things, was that there were a lot of things she would do that would start off seeming normal—you know, they'd be things that normal moms or women would do—but would end up twisted and odd. Like having friends, big festive Christmas parties, or treasuring photographs, or even being so "kind" as to adopt unfortunate little children for instance.

I will never forget my mom's friend Jolene Rossford. This is one of the few people who she called a "friend" who she didn't call that simply because she was waiting for a moment to take them for all they were worth. Jolene was my mom's confidante—her buddy, the person she liked the hang out with and gossip with. On the surface, this seems like a normal, healthy relationship for a woman with children to have. Two women, sitting together in the kitchen talking about their lives and their children—standard mom stuff. Except just like with anything else that could almost pass as normal with my mom, there was something dark—something that sat just under the surface.

Yes, they would sit around and joke and laugh and do normal friend stuff, but from what I remember, the nature of their jokes and source of their conversation usually went along the lines of Jolene saying something like, "Goddamn those kids. I can't stand 'em. Wish I could just get the hell rid of them for good. Unfortunately, you have to take care of them or else you know as well as I do somebody will get in my business and come around looking for them. God knows if I could get away with it I would wash my hands of them this minute. Little bastards." You see at the heart of it, Jolene was someone who had kids just to get the welfare money and live off the state. Blanket statements like this would usually come out after she'd just gotten through beating the hell out of them, which is something that she did on a regular basis like my mom. And just when you'd expect there to be something normal about a conversation like this—you know, where one mother hears this and says to another, "You have to get yourself together; your kids are special—please go get some help," my mother would simply laugh her ass off. She would nod her head in agreement and commiserate with Jolene about it, like they were somehow the victims, like their behavior was perfectly acceptable.

And I remember Jolene Rossford's kids. They were so skinny, like they'd been starved within an inch of their lives. One of the younger children, the one who always had to take care of his siblings, had a broken arm one day because he'd made the baby formula wrong. I knew the look, it was a fear that a kid would project after a beating had just come his way, and the demeanor that radiated from the need or the want to do anything to prevent another one. I knew the look because it was one that I had seen on my own face. His eyes always looked so huge in his head—so big and sunken and sad. There was no spark in them—it had been beaten out over the short course of his life.

And one day Jolene Rossford beat him again, but this time it was until he was dead. And then she didn't know what to do so she shoved his lifeless body under her bed. And as scrawny as the poor kid had been, he was too big to be hidden that easily, so before she chucked him under there to hide him, she made sure to chop him into small pieces. The trash bag held him much easier that way anyway.

This all happened in a building my family owned, and before long, there were some complaints about the smell that was coming from Jolene's unit. My dad and Raymond, responding to Jolene's assertion that the freezer broke and the meat was starting to rot, tried to help her, telling her they'd be glad to take whatever was stinking and get rid of it for her. But she kept saying "no" and the smell of her dead child's dismembered body continued to get worse. Now she really had a problem. But she didn't need to worry—she wasn't alone. Because my mother didn't help her move the body, she never wanted to dirty her hands personally, Jolene eventually turned to her boyfriend for help.

But now, with that, it's time to examine my mother's take on friendship. Perhaps I am getting ahead of myself as I tell this story about my mom and her girlfriend. You see, when friends find themselves in a sticky situation, that's when a friendship sure becomes valuable. And like any good friend, when Jolene Rossford turned to my mom for help, my mom did what any good buddy would do when they found out their friend is in need after killing her child with her bare hands. She saw an opportunity. You see, the moment that my mother learned that Jolene had killed and chopped up her kid, she turned her in. Jolene ended up fleeing town and my mother ended up with an apartment full of belongings, furniture and other goods that she now considered hers, ready for the sale. My mom stalked into that apartment where a young child had been brutally murdered and helped herself to everything in the place. It might have all still had some of the stench of death clinging to it faintly, but no matter.

Eventually, Jolene got in a bar fight and everything unraveled from there. She went to prison where, coincidentally enough, the two—my mom and Jolene—would meet again years later.

Mom was just doing what any good buddy would do for

another. And when the two ladies met again behind bars, in prison like in the real world, they were the best of friends. Still are, as a matter of fact.

So yeah, in addition to all the city councilmen, elected officials, and other people of importance who graced my mom's front steps, these are the kinds of people who came into our home.

THE SAINTS OF SPRING STREET...

We hadn't lived in our house on Spring Street long before mom, who already had her hands full with my brother Bruce, who was born in 1972, decided that she wanted to have another daughter. At this time, the family "business" wasn't anything like the robust enterprise it would later become. At that point in time, my mom was still working out her system to get anything and everything possible as cheap as she could so she could make money on the apartments. After all, that was the whole beginning of her shoplifting habit (although "habit" is probably far too mild of a word to use when describing what she did). She didn't steal then for any purpose outside of her desire to cut her costs so she could make more money on the apartments.

Anyway, at this time Bruce was just a little over a year-old when mom decided that he needed someone to play with who was around his age—someone to grow up with and hang around other than Candace. It just so happened that she was able to quickly get what she wanted without bothering with all the trouble of giving birth herself or mess with any long drawn-out formal proceedings to adopt a foster child through the state system.

There was a tenant on Johnson Street who knew a young nineteen-year old named Lisa who just had a baby and was having a hard time taking care of her. She was struggling without any support from her parents or friends and was moving from house to house. The baby had been born out of wedlock and no one wanted anything to do with her.

One afternoon, my dad and I were at the Johnson Street house; I was running in and out playing while he worked to fix a problem in the home. Evidently, he heard the woman talking to someone about this poor Lisa girl and her baby girl and got wind of the idea that the girl was desperate to do something since she was having such trouble taking care of the baby. Immediately sensing an opportunity, my dad chimed in that he would be more than willing to help the poor girl out.

My dad was kind enough to meet with the poor girl and listen to her troubles. Her began by soothing her and letting her know that everything was going to be okay—that all she needed was some time to get back on her feet. "Why don't you let us take care of her for a while—just to give you time to save some money and get yourself together?", he asked her after explaining all that she'd be able to do if she just had some time to collect herself and get something better going on for herself.

Lisa thought about this for a moment but refused at first, saying "I don't want to give her up or anything—she's my child. I just need some help for a little while, something temporary."

My dad nodded in agreement, looking sympathetic, patting her shoulder. "Of course," he said.

Lisa thought about my dad's offer for help for a few days before she finally came out to the house to see if it was really something she wanted. She was nervous but knew it would be temporary. All the while during her visit my parents talked to her about all the great things she'd be able to do with this little break in her life—college, jobs, moving on and finding something stable so she could give her infant daughter, whose name was Hope*, a good life. They sold her on the idea that all she needed was just a little time to get her life in order—and that they were the folks who could help her get there. Out of the kindness of their hearts, of course.

My mother put on one hell of a show that day. And I can't blame Lisa for falling for it, either. After all, she was swept away after having her head filled with hopeful thoughts about all she could accomplish and was even more blown away by the presentation she was given of the home and the family who inhabited it. Her visit was a whirlwind—it swirled her out of her senses. She toured through our sixteen-room, sprawling, beautifully-furnished home—all the while listening to my mother prattle on endlessly, delightedly about all of the luxuries that her baby daughter would have access to, including an enormous space that would be her very own special bedroom.

And what was Lisa thinking as she was danced about the home, filled with visions of a glorious, stable future? All I can imagine that went through her head was, *What a perfect home! What a perfect, amazing family! What saints these people are—to be so privileged yet so willing to help someone like me!*

And you know, it's hard to find Lisa completely guilty of ignorance with an actress as good as my mother on the grand tour, leading her through our home—smiling, playing the part of the matron saint. And like the desperate single mother she was, she did the only thing she could at the time, she agreed to let her daughter stay with what seemed like the perfect family while she got on her feet. When she left that day she was tearful and sad, but a faint glimmer of relief and some envy for the lifestyle she expected her child to have flickered across her face as well.

She felt that she was doing the right thing, after all. No matter how much it hurt her to leave her Hope behind. Just for a while…

*Hope's name was later changed.

*   *   *   *   *

There's No Hope Here...

If I've learned anything in life, it's there there's no such thing as getting something for nothing. Like most people, I've learned it the hard way but I can think of few other people who learned that lesson quite as harshly as Lisa did when she left baby Hope in my mother's "temporary" care.

My mother took to the little girl immediately, cooing and fussing over her. She did, however, refuse to call the girl Hope and forbade any of us to do it either. She hated that name but I imagine, even from the moment she gave Lisa her first tour of the house, Mom was running through her mental list of favorite baby names so she could pick the right one for when this little girl became her own. I don't know when she actually chose the name "Rachel" but something tells me it was sometime around the moment Lisa agreed to let Mom watch Hope for a while.

One afternoon, not too long after Lisa left her baby Hope with us, my mom told her to meet her at the office of our family's attorney so that she could have Lisa sign some papers that would allow her infant daughter to be on our family's health insurance plan. I can only imagine how pleased Lisa was that day to hurry along to meet Mom and her lawyer to sign her daughter up for some quality healthcare. They sat there and chatted, very casual, making sure that Lisa didn't pay too close attention to what she was signing and parted ways on great terms that afternoon, with full promises of great doctors and good health.

I imagine Lisa walked away that day completely convinced that her little Hope couldn't have ended up with better temporary caregivers. I imagine she felt her future was bright that day. I imagine she wondered how she could be getting so many amazing benefits for her daughter for nothing.

But while there have been a clause or two about medical care in the long document Lisa had to sign in a few places as she sat there, lightheartedly talking with my mother and our family lawyer, the nature of those papers entailed far more than just medical insurance responsibility. What Lisa signed that afternoon was a full set of adoption papers—legal to the "t" and with her signature emblazoned permanently and in ink on each dotted line she'd been distractedly asked to sign.

If Lisa had looked closely at that paperwork instead of trusting in her matron saint Frances, she also would have noticed that the papers clearly stated that from that day on the child's name would legally be "Rachel Lynn Burt."

*   *   *   *   *

A couple of days after their meeting with the attorney, Lisa stopped by to visit with my mother and her little Hope, just as she had been doing since she left Hope in my family's care the first time. As far as Lisa knew, the meeting with the lawyer was a formality to keep her daughter healthy—she had no idea that anything had changed.

She walked up to the door and knocked her usual, timid knock. My mother answered the door, a cold, hard look on her face. "What in the hell do you want?" she said, glaring at Lisa like she was a filthy bum who had come begging—like a stranger.

Lisa looked shocked. She had no idea what to think. "I...I...I came to see Hope," she stammered, confused and beginning to shake.

My mother narrowed her steely eyes and looked straight into Lisa's. "There's no Hope here," she said coldly.

That chilling statement echoed in her ears, it made no sense to Lisa. She searched my mother's hard eyes for some sign, some clue that she was joking, but found nothing except a defiant, brutal blankness staring back.

Not knowing what else to do, not fully comprehending what had happened, Lisa began to cry, she had no idea what it meant, "there's no Hope here," and figured there must be some kind of misunderstanding. She weakly tried to explain to my mother—to tell her—who Hope was; that Hope was the baby and why, oh why, did my mom keep telling her that Hope wasn't there? If she wasn't there, where was she, and why in the hell didn't mom act like she even recognized her at all?

"There is no Hope here," repeated my mother, spitting out her words as if the name itself had a terrible taste. "You gave up your rights, I changed her name and she is ours, so get off my property, peanut butter legs, before I have the cops remove you."

She slammed the door in Lisa's face.

I imagine Lisa must have stood there for a long time before it sunk in what had happened. Before the vast, unimaginable reality of what my mother, with her eyes like tiny, glazed stones, was saying.

But it started to seep into her, that horrible, sinking realization. It took a few minutes before her body started to look like a heavy weight had suddenly descended and came to rest on her shoulders. And then she started wailing—incoherent, pained cries. I remember her screaming in the street and my mother once screaming back at her, mocking her, calling her "peanut butter legs" over and over—an expression that was one of her favorites for defining a loose woman, a woman whose legs spread as easily as peanut butter. And Lisa screamed on and on, helpless anguish in her throaty, tortured roars. She would often grow exhausted and overcome, would lean on the chain-link fence (which we would eventually replace with a stockade fence, which gave our property the appearance of a revolutionary fort or a compound) and cry endless tears.

My mother would pretend she wasn't there after a while. It was even easier to do after it became clear that nothing would ever make her relinquish control of her new little daughter. And people did try, damn hard too, to get Lisa's daughter back safely to her, but to no avail. After all, a signature was a signature. Rachel's grandparents tried for years to keep the courts fresh on the case, hoping against hope that their granddaughter would be returned. Despite the fact that it was clear some coercion was used to get Lisa to sign the papers, none of that could be proven and the case for Hope died with each decision.

This little event actually made history. It was the first time a natural mother lost her child in favor of adoptive parents.

The case was traumatic and Lisa Overton, that poor, desperate young mother faced nothing but the cruelest insults from my family. If asked about her today, my mother, would undoubtedly laugh at her stupidity, "dumb, begging little peanut butter legs," she'd say, chuckling that empty little laugh that chills me to the bone just to think about.

Like adopted kids do, Rachel had a certain curiosity about where she came from. She used to ask about her real mom when she got older; she knew that she had been taken in, but had no idea what the true circumstances were fully at that time. She found out some of the story when she was thirteen or fourteen and mom would field her questions with ease. "Oh, you were a mess; you were malnourished, near death. Your mom was horrible—she used to beat you! You are damn lucky that I was there to save your life."

Mom would take on the role of the saint again, making Rachel feel like she'd done her the most marvelous favor. But like all of the kids, adopted or not, Mom made sure financial dependence guaranteed loyalty to her. Rachel, like the rest of us, ended up being wholly financially dependent on my parents and even though she did run away three times, she was always brought back. You can't run away from our family. There is no way out. The only way out for my wife and I was the route we took with the help of the state police. Somehow though, Rachel always carried around some twisted sense of owing my parents—of feeling dedicated to them, even after she'd been treated like a dog and her natural mother had been treated even worse. When dad got out of jail, sure enough, Rachel was at his side—she'd go and spend weeks at a time with them. And to me, it's sick beyond words, she even named her first-born after my father.

As backwards as it all might seem to an outsider that there would still be any loyalty to my parents after everything she went through, and knowing at least a good part of what her mom dealt with, I can only say that this is just another shred of irrefutable proof of the persuasive power of Frances Burt. As soon as she saw someone slipping through her fingers, she'd pull out that magical trump card—guilt. Guilt alone binds Rachel to them. It's a searing sense of guilt so strong that no amount of abuse or torture could recondition or un-brainwash her.

Rachel is really the only person from my family that I would have contact with after everyone was thrown in jail. In the years since then, as we've talked about what happened to us, she talked in great detail about all of the times my father raped her. When she calls out her son's name, I wonder to what extent it hits her—if at all—just how dark it is that she would name her child after the man who took his sickness out on her and all the other adopted kids in that house. But I know she has been conditioned and I am sad for her, just as I am sad for all of us.

NADINE

Satisfied that now she had the daughter she wanted without the pain and hassle of bothering with giving birth herself (and with surprisingly easy legal battles that always turned in her favor), mom set her focus on making money with the apartments. She had a nose for sniffing out weakness, especially when it came to tenants, and knew how to exploit and twist anything and everything possible in order to make an extra buck. If she knew someone in one of the apartments needed an electric space heater, for instance, she would be more than happy to volunteer to provide one at a low monthly cost. But this cost came with interest and a rental fee and before the poor renter knew it, he'd be paying triple the cost of what it would take to buy a new one over the course of several months of her rental and interest fees. Lots of people owed my mom and believe me, she always found a way to extract whatever she was owed—and then some—when all was said and done.

Around the time Rachel came to live with us, my mom rented out an apartment to a woman whom she knew immediately would be the perfect person for the space. She was exactly the type of tenant my mother liked to have—slow-witted, gullible, and ridiculously easy to manipulate. To her, meeting Nadine was just about as good as having a pile of money thrown into her lap—it was all too simple.

My mother had a sixth sense about people and knew before they opened their mouths for the first time whether or not they'd be someone she would be able to use, to take for everything he or she was worth and then some. If she could, she'd usually start in on them right away, and if they weren't, well, God forbid they had anything to do with the family or their lives would be miserable. Arlean would be able to tell you all about that.

From the moment she came to check the place out, Nadine Carpenter was one of those easy targets my mom had a knack for picking out. Sniffling, meek, humble Nadine—if only she'd known what she was walking into that day she came seeking an apartment. Like so many others who've fallen into a trap of some kind my mother carefully but casually laid, I often wonder how many nights were spent laying awake cursing the day she ever met any of us Burts.

Smelling weakness like a hungry carrion feeder sniffs out untouched road kill, my mother started her work on Nadine immediately. This one was just too easy and juicy for her to risk losing. As was her custom with weak and desperate women, phase one of the "program" for getting someone like Nadine in line began with ultimate kindness. It's hard to imagine, especially knowing that she'd eventually become a prisoner, a hostage, really in almost every sense, but it all began with niceties and pleasantries. My mother, in her first meetings with Nadine, started by treating her with sickly sweet kindness, knowing that a woman like her would bend to her will, whether she actively wanted to or not. This was the exact same tactic she used to get Rachel—by putting on the "saint show" and making her victim feel like Mrs. Burt could do no wrong. Like Lisa Overton, the slow Nadine never saw anything coming and when it finally did start, she was so trapped that there was no way for her to claw her way out.

Yes, my mother likely took note of a few things about Nadine Carpenter right away as she sized her up for her net worth. Her face wore a look of constant vacancy, which showed in the form of a vague half-smile when she was preoccupied. She also jotted down a mental note that Nadine was very religious and, as my mother knew, religious people could always be manipulated. My mother also decided, probably right away, that it would be no trouble at all to get not only Nadine wrapped around her finger, but the hodge-podge lot of family that came with her.

Nadine wasn't renting the apartment for herself alone; she had a boyfriend, Luke, who was also not "all there" as most people would say, and she also had four children of varying ages—Marie, Ricky, LeeAnn, and L.J. If these kids had any idea of what their lives were going to be like after meeting the Burts, they probably would have run away without looking back at the very thought of it. By the time a couple of them did run, it was already far too late.

Marie was a few years older than I was, Ricky and I were about the same age, LeeAnn was Rachel's age and L.J. was much younger. I know my mom wondered how this woman who was, as it was clear to nearly anyone who met her, very slow, could raise four kids, especially since she didn't work.

Knowing all about how women like Nadine got by after years spent dealing with tenants in the apartments, my mom was sure that Nadine probably was on welfare and Social Security. From her perspective, this absolutely was enough to get Nadine the apartment—my mom loved it when tenants got public dollars every month because it was guaranteed income that they couldn't claim didn't exist. In other words, while a lot of them were what she considered "trash", the people on government assistance were her favorite kinds of renters.

Nadine was some of the easiest prey Mom could have imagined and from the beginning, from her first few loans, Nadine had little idea what she was getting herself into. It started off simply enough; Nadine would be short on money and knew mom would always be glad to lend her a few bucks here and there—with interest, of course. At the beginning of the month, she might borrow $5 or $10 from mom, which by the end of the month, when the interest was tacked on, that amount would become double, which oftentimes meant that Nadine would have to take out yet another loan at the beginning of the next month. In no time, she had herself in a hole—just from these very small loans that eventually ended up amounting to far more than Nadine could afford. It was usury at its worst but my mom was always more than happy to lend and Nadine, perhaps because she figured that in the end God would make sure things worked out in her favor (or maybe simply because she just wasn't smart enough to figure out what was going on), was always fine with borrowing just a little more. After all, to her, how could $5 loans sporadically land her in the hole?

Coupled with the loan repayments with their ridiculous interest levels, Nadine also found herself needing some things for her apartment that my mom was also glad to supply at a small monthly cost. For instance, with four kids and Luke and the knowledge that if she needed anything it would be given (even if it was something she lived without for a long time before) Nadine decided she needed a washer and dryer to keep up with her laundry. With a single word to my mom about the issue, in no time a washer and dryer from one of the other apartments (which was probably stolen from the tenants on one shaky pretense or another) was dispatched. It seemed very reasonable to Nadine that there would be a monthly charge but it never occurred to her that with the amount she was paying monthly, she could have saved up that fee for a few months and bought her own for a fraction of what she eventually ended up paying my mom over the course of several months. It just never occurred to her. It's like she lived in a fairy land most of the time—one where God watched out for her so she didn't need to bother with things like worrying about how she was being a victim of some pretty bold usury.

This was a system with mom and her tenants. Countless numbers of them owed her money each month for things as small as tiny loans of $10 to the fees for appliances and other things tenants considered necessities. This system paid well, especially considering that there were so many people who were paying interest or other fees for things she got for free anyway or had no problem giving. It was a beautiful thing to her—making money off of things that were free. Anytime she could find something for nothing and then pass it off for a charge of some kind she was delighted. For someone whose heart was never touched by happiness about anything else—family, children, love—this was the one salvation; the bright spot.

But out of all people, Nadine was the victim of this to the greatest extent. Within a very short period of time after meeting my mom and moving in, the poor lady's entire check was gone the moment she got it. Every single cent went to my mom and then she just had to borrow more to keep afloat while living with the bare minimum. Nadine struggled on and I wonder when and if it ever occurred to her just what kind of hole she'd dug with herself. After all, when Frances Burt was involved, it's not like there would ever be any way out.

Seeing another opportunity, my mom started to take Nadine's pre-teen daughter, Marie, under her wing, beginning, of course, with her usual tactic of sweetness and generosity—playing the matron saint again. Although it started out as a special thing when Marie first started staying overnight at our house, ostensibly to hang out with Candace, it became more frequent. My mom started to actively encourage Marie to stay over at our house, making sure to point out how much better it was at the Burt house than at her own. It's not like it was difficult since Marie was at an age anyway when a girl starts to rebel against her parents, but when my mom really started in on Marie in her effort to make her see her "other" life as sad and worthless, it didn't take long until Marie just stayed permanently—she didn't ever want to leave. Nadine missed Marie and didn't necessarily want her living at our house, but what could she really say about it? After all, by the time Marie had become a fixture at our place Nadine was up to her neck in debt to my mom and far too weak-willed and meek to actually confront my mother about it. It just became, like so many other sick things in our house, "the way things were" and if it's a way that my mom had designated things to be there wasn't a damn thing anybody—anybody at all—could do about it.

The longer Marie stayed, the more she started to think that her other life with her mom was shitty. And the longer Marie stayed, the more she was exposed to my mom's influence. And the more this influence crept into her soul—a soul that longed more than anything to be a Burt—the more she turned sour. Within a relatively short period, especially after getting the (false) feeling that my mom loved her more than her mother ever could, my mom's bad-mouthing of Nadine rubbed off on Marie. And actually, more than just rubbing off, I am quite sure my mom taught Marie to call her mom names—names like "retard," for instance, which became everyone's favorite word when they wanted Nadine to come running, which sadly, she always did.

More than just teaching Marie to call her own mother nasty

things, my mom had little trouble teaching Marie to hit her mom. Like my mother, Marie also preferred slapping Nadine across the face or hitting her on the head with blunt objects.

You see, this became easy for my mom and Marie to do because after a while, Nadine was so in debt to my mom that she became our house slave. And there is no exaggeration when I use the word "slave" either. Nadine was required to do anything my mother asked and while this included almost all the housework, it also meant she was to be ready at the command whenever my mom wanted anything that she didn't feel like doing herself. And I'd like to say that Nadine was only beaten when she didn't do a good job or failed to perform to my mom's expectations, but that's not at all true. My mom and Nadine's own daughter, Marie, beat the hell out of Nadine on a pretty regular basis. It didn't matter at all if Nadine had done something wrong—which she often didn't, she did prove to be an excellent housekeeper, although the constant looming threat of violence might have had something to do with that. If my mom or Marie were having a bad day, Nadine was the scapegoat.

I can't count how many times Nadine got racked over the head with a dull object. She didn't seem to mind much getting slapped in the face or hit in other ways, but man, when my mom or Marie would take a knick-knack off the shelf and bash her over the head with it, she'd always react, rolling on the floor, wailing, holding her head and screaming like she thought she was going to die. This reaction almost seemed like something she couldn't help. She couldn't stand being hit on the head, which often meant that my mom or Marie would just do it more often. After a while, seeing that this was just a regular reaction, they started to think it was funny—this dramatic reaction to being bashed in the head—and they'd do that more often. My mom would sometimes get pissed off that Nadine was wailing so loudly though and would start kicking her while she laid on the ground, rolling about and moaning.

This went on for years and years. My mom never got tired

of it. And for that matter, Marie never seemed to tire of it much either and was always the first to chime in when someone, usually my mom, called her mother a retard.

You see, none of it was hard for Marie then. She had everything she'd always wanted—and her needs were pretty basic, especially after living in cramped quarters with her entire family for so many years. As soon as my mother started working on turning Marie against her mother, she bent. My mom seemed to instinctively know what would most appeal to Marie—what would most get her to want to stay. She wanted her own room. Her very own bedroom. After all, what teenage girl wouldn't? She also wanted to be a Burt. To her, we were glamorous, rich, beyond reproach. She wanted to be like Candace—she wanted to be Marie Burt—and my mother was able to feed that. From the beginning, she told Marie she wanted to adopt her, to get her away from her retarded mother and into a place that she deserved. She fed her most basic desires and it didn't take much to get Marie to respond.

My mother became like the mother that Marie wanted. She did a few things that made Marie happy, including teaching her to cook. For weeks on end, my mother did something she wouldn't have done with any of her own girls—she went into the kitchen and with great care and deliberation, patiently showed Marie everything that was involved in running a kitchen and cooking for a big family. She made Marie love it. To anyone passing through our house at that time who had no knowledge of anything that was going on, the scene could have been plucked out of a home and garden or family magazine; a nice big, airy kitchen and a mother and daughter, smiling and working on a menu to delight the family.

But like everything else in our family, this was a total farce. My mom could not have given a shit less about being a good parent or mother figure. Just as was the case with anything else she did that might make it seem to an outsider like she was showing love or affection, the ultimate function behind her cooking sessions with Marie was purely selfish. She was training Marie for a life of slavery. Mom already had Nadine as a house slave to do the chores, but what mom really wanted was a kitchen slave—someone whose only task was to prepare the meals and keep the kitchen clean, which was always an undertaking with so many people in the house.

And so it was. Marie was the kitchen slave, her mother, abused and dejected, was the housekeeper. They were not paid, but at least they had a roof over their heads.

At the beginning, even as it might have just started to dawn on her at the tender age of 14 that she was nothing to the family outside of the kitchen slave, Marie felt like she had it made. She had herself convinced that now that she was a "Burt" in the sense that she lived in our house, that her life was about as good as it was ever going to get. She dropped out of school as soon as she was able and you'd better believe this made my mom about as happy as could be. After all, who was going to make lunches and keep up with the dishes if Marie was at school?

To keep Marie, my mom caught on quickly to what got her going. She figured out in no time that Marie would be content if she felt like she had a little bit of power or control. Mom also realized that the best way to give Marie some feeling that she was powerful while also serving her own twisted ends was to tell Marie that her mother, Nadine, worked for her. She told Marie this a lot at the beginning and also made it clear to her that if Nadine screwed something up, she needed to be beaten. She would demonstrate, slapping Nadine, calling her names, hitting her over the head and making blood run from her temples.

She gave Marie a little bat once and told her that her mom was a retard—that she'd fucked something up—that she was an idiot who didn't deserve any better. Mom stood there laughing as Marie, without a look of remorse of consciousness about what she was doing, took the bat and beat the hell out of Nadine. She felt powerful and more importantly, for that moment, she gained my mother's unwavering approval.

She denied all of this when she appeared on television to talk about what had happened, she never went to jail, and probably still would to this day, but she was one of the most savage abusers of Nadine. One of the most violent.

My mom really got Marie—she had her tightly wrapped and molded into exactly what she wanted. And Marie didn't complain for a long time, you see because then, it was enough for her. No more school to bother with and she had her very own special room and that was the most important thing. I don't know how long it was after she'd moved in for good that my dad started raping her repeatedly, but something tells me it didn't take him long to smell the fresh meat. He was glad she had her own room, too.

Life went on for us with the mother and daughter helping to keep up the house and kitchen. And for a long time, neither of them complained, except for Nadine when she'd get hit so hard by either her daughter or my mom that blood would trickle down the sides of her face in little dark streams. Then she'd wail, but once she was over it, she'd be right back at it— cleaning and running around the house getting her chores done.

Nadine's son, Ricky, who was much closer to my own age, also was taken in by the family; my father taught him from a young age the ins and outs of working on apartments because, after all, it was free help and he could get away from the family he'd been taught to despise, too. Nadine would always go to Ricky and Marie for help, but their reaction was always the same, "You're not my mother," coupled with a spiteful, cold look.

Soon enough, the simple claims of "You're not my mother" turned into more hateful things to say to Nadine without basis. My mom saw the value and gain these kids could provide and took her case to the Department of Child Welfare. As a land-lady, she had ample paperwork and other proof that Nadine and her boyfriend Luke couldn't afford the burden of their four children. She also demonstrated to the agency that they were mentally unfit to be parents and that she would be a much better parent as she had the means and the presumed mental health to raise them the way they should be brought up.

There was little fight from the Department of Child Welfare; my mother was convincing and may have actually had a few valid points in the case she made. The only thing that Nadine and Luke had to offer their children was love, but what does that matter to an agency or to my mom? You guessed it—not shit.

Our family grew that year, first with Marie and Ricky, and then also by the addition of young LeeAnn and little L.J.

And yes, I imagine you're probably wondering why in the hell Nadine never got out—why she never would have tried to make a break for it. The answer is simple. Because no matter what kind of verbal or physical abuse her daughter Marie or son Ricky laid on her, no matter how many times they told their mother she wished she would die, that she was nothing but a retard, Nadine was their mother. And like any good, caring mother, she would not leave her kids. Nadine stayed because she could not bear to lose her children, and even though they were in the same house with their mother for years and years to come, she was as good as gone.

But just as importantly, my mom made it perfectly clear when Nadine cried about her lost children that she was always welcome to see them at the house. So it stood—she became a house slave to be around her children who, unbeknownst to them, had also become slaves—in one way or another. Nadine couldn't bear to leave them, no matter how she was treated. She would put up with any abuse just to be near them, even though they pushed her off when she'd tried to talk to them or show them any kind of affection. Her boyfriend Luke stayed too, because after all, where was he going to go? Like Nadine, Luke had a weak will and tended to roll with the punches.

So after the formal adoption and the new house help from Nadine and Luke and his boys to assist my dad, my parents couldn't have been more pleased. Because all in all, my parents benefitted enormously from the Carpenters. Free kitchen, house, and apartment help—there were no costs to them. Only pure net gain.

Little goldmines, all of them.

THE STRANGLEHOLD

It's often hard for people outside of my family to believe that my mom could have such an influence on people, but believe it. It was rare for her to encounter someone—anyone—whom she couldn't twist and bend to her will. The stupider, less wise or street-smart someone was, the better she "liked" them.

As I've already made clear, Nadine and Luke were exactly the type of people my mom wanted to know—slow-witted and dull, accepting of their fates with minimal outbursts bemoaning their states in life. God made it all possible for my mom—at least in the sense that God became the perfect tool to use against Nadine when nothing else was working. You see, in Nadine's eyes, anything and everything that happened was God's will. Whenever mom saw Nadine's ability to accept what was happening start to slide, all she needed to do was invoke the Lord's name and remind her that it was all part of God's great, mysterious plan and resignedly, weakly, Nadine would fall back in line.

My mom couldn't risk losing her stranglehold over the Carpenters—they were among her most valuable, multi-functional possessions. The free house and kitchen work was great, but they also came with other side benefits—ones that probably helped me stay healthy, now that I look back on it.

I remember once wondering why, when it was time to go to the doctor or the dentist, my mom always made me tell the doctor that my name was "Ricky" instead of "Randy." She was always clear and insisted on it, using threats to keep me from forgetting. "Remember, your name is Ricky," she'd say with that powerful glare that meant, "if you forget there'll be some serious hell to pay", and off I'd trot. After a while, when I was told to do something like that, I never thought twice about it. It was normal to say I was someone else anytime I went somewhere.

Of course I believe my mother was committing Medicaid fraud based upon the fact that while my teeth were nice and clean with fillings when I had cavities, Ricky and Marie's teeth were allowed to rot. I know from first hand experience that when I got sick or needed medical attention, I was always rushed off to the doctor without a fuss, but when Ricky or Marie took ill, they were hidden away in bed and denied treatment. This wasn't just because my mom didn't care (because make no mistake about it—she didn't, as long as they were going to live through whatever ailed them) it was because she used the state-funded medical and dental care that is provided for foster children on me and my siblings. Just as I was told I was Ricky, Candace was to call herself Marie at the doctor's— and so it went for years and years.

When I say that the Carpenters were goldmines, it goes even further than the free medical care for us. With Nadine at our house and at my mother's service full-time, she had no need for her welfare checks. At first, Nadine would just go cash them herself and give the money to my mom, but over time, my mom decided to forgo that delay on her funds and became the legal recipient of their state checks. How? Simple, by presenting Nadine and Luke as mentally incompetent and unmarried. There was really nothing to it for someone with the persuasive power my mom possessed. It was ridiculously, sinfully easy.

In addition to the monthly checks that were supposed to provide support for Nadine and Luke to live on, the child welfare system also came with a boatload of funding. Monthly checks for care and school supplies (which were completely unneeded since school was only something they did to fulfill legal requirements, then they were allowed to drop out) and for Christmas presents too. The benefits were endless.

Speaking of Christmas, it was ridiculous—it was like a free-for-all. My mom would get an influx of cash from the state for Christmas presents and on top of that, since she was just beginning to take her shoplifting to a new level she was getting free items through ill-gotten means. She would also encourage all of the kids to go steal their own presents, so she wouldn't have to spend a dime. Christmas would be free for her and sometimes she'd even make money off of the holiday. Most of the presents she'd get for the foster kids would be stolen and, while she'd spend some of their Christmas money from the state on us, we'd also get stolen stuff too so she'd be able to pocket a nice chunk of the cash at the end of the holiday and keep everyone feeling like they'd gotten something at the same time.

What a lovely thing it was to her. Christmas grew increasingly ridiculous year after year, each holiday season bigger than the last, but at this point, things were just really starting to roll. And it was all thanks to her little goldmines, each and every member of the Carpenter family.

Outside of the cash and medical care, my mom was able to extract something else of particular value from the whole thing. Knowledge—a deep understanding of just what was possible when foster kids were concerned. Through Nadine's children (all of the kids were not Luke's children) my mom quickly realized how valuable foster children could be. They would be natural servants in the house with only minimal incentives if they'd been deprived for most of their lives—a private room or feeling of belonging. And the checks—oh, the big checks. My parents were making money right and left on the apartments and now the kids were an added source of wealth in cash and in work.

Since they couldn't pay rent anyway and had become such a useful set of possessions, my mom moved Nadine and her boyfriend Luke into a tiny little windowless room in the basement. Nadine was glad that she would be able to be near her kids and Luke, well, what choice did he have? They had some sparse furnishing down there—enough to keep them from complaining, and from that point on we had live-in servants. Before that, the two had to walk thirty minutes every day to get to "work" so at least this kept them from ever being late too, not to mention the added convenience of my mom being able to scream at Nadine anytime she needed something during hours Nadine might otherwise have been away.

It was a brilliant course of events for Mom; life was good. Now she had straight-up cash *and* live-in house slaves. And my father had his own special sort of slaves too. The stranglehold was pure and complete and with time, a grim sort of acceptance set in and all of this—the foster children, the slavery—it all became "normal" to us.

But, of course, there was nothing normal about us or anything that happened after they became part of our family. It even sounds wrong to say that they did become part of the Burt clan—it's more like they were there because that's where we told them to be. Over time, they all settled into what would become their positions in the house and there was some form of "procedure." All of those kids; all four of them had something about them that wasn't quite right—they weren't all there in one way or another. I guess it's not hard to imagine considering who their parents were, but they did have quirks.

*   *   *   *   *

The Extended Family

Our family grew and soon, despite the grim circumstances that led everyone to their positions and into new lives, some sense of acceptance settled over everyone. The children and even Nadine and Luke in their dim basement accommodations settled in. A routine, a norm was passively established.

Marie was one of the first to fall into position and hers was, as you might imagine, in the kitchen. In fact, that position became so ingrained in her that I hardly remember seeing her anywhere but the kitchen. For a long time though, I will say that she seemed to enjoy or at least readily accept the fact that she was the kitchen slave. She seemed comfortable there and anytime she was away from the food and pots and pans she'd seem awkward—out of place. I don't know if she liked that at certain times of the day she'd be where the action was, since the kitchen was often the hub, or if it's just that she didn't know where else she belonged, but she remained there, day in and day out. I think part of her was always trying to get back to those days she spent with my mother—who then seemed like a dream mom to her. It was as if hard work in the kitchen might somehow make Mom notice she was there. My mom really didn't notice her after a while though. Sometimes she'd take time out of her day to beat her if something had gone wrong, but for the most part, Mom just let her alone after she was sure she wasn't going anywhere. The only time that Mom would ever really pay any attention to Marie was when she would instruct her to beat Nadine. It was strange and dark, but it was like they bonded through this one particular thing. When Mom would turn her rage on Marie, I think Marie took it easily because at least it was some kind of attention, even if it was negative.

At about the same time Marie settled into the kitchen and became as permanent as the refrigerator in there, she was to the point where she'd beat Nadine if Nadine dared to mention, even offhand, that she was her mother. Sometimes Nadine would come into the kitchen to see her, but after a while, she learned and didn't bother. One afternoon, just for fun, Marie got a handful of earthworms and put them on Nadine's sandwich. When my mother saw what happened she laughed right along with Marie the whole time.

Outside of a few rare events, in my memory, I can't see Marie outside of the kitchen. She'd make drinks, clean up after us—she'd pretty much do anything we asked without complaint. Eventually she would come to realize what had been happening and start to rail against it, but it really was too late by that time. It was too late for any of them once the full realization of their lives crept up and bit them.

Ricky also settled into his new life as part (but not) of the family. He was quiet and reserved, obedient. We got along well and were friendly while growing up and my dad certainly made great use of him. He was a hard worker and was the best free help Dad could have ever had on the apartments. After all, anyone else doing the kind of work that Ricky did would have to be paid, and who would want to actually pay someone when you get something for free? Ricky and L.J. put in so many hundreds of free working hours for my dad that a lifetime of Dad trying to repay them, even minimum wage, wouldn't be possible. My mom wasn't the only one, after all, who knew something about slavery.

LeeAnn was the one who suffered the most and in some ways, I think she was victimized even more than her mother was. Out of all four of those kids, all of which had something about them that might be called "slow," LeeAnn was by far the most mentally challenged. She was younger than us and this probably made her easier to get at. I always felt sorry for her; she was so quiet—hardly ever said a word to anyone. She seemed to live in a state of perpetual fear. She reminded me of a dull-witted, abused little kitten, always around, lurking, afraid of what was going to come next. When she wasn't scurrying to get away from everyone, she had a habit of sitting in a chair, rocking until she hit her own head. She would mumble as she did this, very low, for hours and hours, almost trance-like. Her eyes would be staring and vacant, there was just nothing there.

It was kind of like a chain or a cycle, but there was always somebody beating on somebody in the house. If Marie left the kitchen, you could be sure she'd be beating her mom, but her other favorite target for abuse became her sister, LeeAnn. I guess it made it easy for her to beat the hell out of her helpless, mentally disabled little sister because it let her feel like she had a bit of power. Whatever the reason was, she did beat her, which only served to make LeeAnn even more frightened and blank. LeeAnn would just take it—she didn't have it in her to fight back. The whole sad affair made me always see LeeAnn like a little animal everyone took their sicknesses out on. The movie got it wrong in this aspect, because it painted Marie as some sort of good person, this saintly character, and really, she was just as brutal as everyone else, especially when she victimized her own family members.

My dad became a regular visitor to LeeAnn's room, she shared it with Rachel. Both girls suffered at his hands. Rachel was raped from the time she was six years old until when she finally left to get married and poor LeeAnn was raped from the moment she entered the house until the time she finally was removed from the house when she was 16. While Rachel made repeated allegations against my dad about the sexual abuse, LeeAnn never said anything, therefore, it happened all the time with her because she was just a warm body with nothing behind her eyes to look at him with. Rachel told me once that she remembers laying awake at night, waiting to hear the familiar steps of my dad coming in. She would pray and pray that he would go to LeeAnn and not her and recalls my dad sitting there with LeeAnn, telling her she was beautiful, doing his business, and then leaving. Rachel told me that every night it was kind of a crapshoot but almost each night, one of them would get a visit. So, it can be said, it wasn't just Mom who stood to gain from the Carpenter clan in the house by any means.

Dad also made good use out of Luke and Nadine. He liked that Luke was a slow but steady and reliable worker, but he also liked that he could get Luke to do just about anything for his amusement. Luke was, like a lot of people who are dim-witted, pretty easy to take advantage of and trick into doing just about anything. I can't count how many times Dad would make Luke do something idiotic (and often dangerous) for a laugh.

I remember this one time I went up to one of the apartments to get my dad for something or another. He was up at one of the places we owned on Bullock Street—a big house with three stories. I climbed the stairs looking for him and kept going up because I thought I heard someone laughing. Sure enough, as I came to the top of the stairs and peered through an opening that looked into a small room on the third floor. I saw my dad and Fred. They were crouched down together, malicious smiles on their faces. They had Nadine stripped naked on the chilly, dirty floor and had Luke perched with his face between her legs. He looked like he was about ready to cry. "I don't want to lick it," he whined, a distasteful look on his face. This admission sent dad and Fred into a laughing fit and they kept egging him on, trying to get him to do something he obviously wasn't familiar with and didn't want to do. They kept coercing him to perform other sexual acts on her and I watched, fully aware of the sickness of the moment, but hoping to get out of there without being noticed.

I knew that Fred and my dad were making the couple perform for them, which is sick in its own right because neither of them really knew any better. Just as I was about to turn away in disgust, Dad spotted me and scrambled to his feet. Before I could run, he snatched me off the stairs and smacked me. He told me to get the hell out of that house and that if I ever told anyone, he'd kill me.

I turned and ran, trying to block what I saw out of my mind, but it's just one of those things a kid can't forget. Unfortunately for me, almost everything I remember from the time I was old enough to have memories comes at me like that memory does—unwelcome and with full force. It's no wonder I can't sleep.

Nadine, beaten by her own children if she called herself

their mother and Luke, too slow to realize that he was the butt of a joke that never ended lived for a long time at the mercy of my parents' whims.

I hate to imagine the other kinds of sexual humiliation Nadine in particular suffered through. Both of my parents got a kick out of her awkward homeliness and enjoyed putting her on the spot and making her squirm. The thing is though, I think that like Marie, Nadine didn't mind being humiliated if she was the center of attention. If she made my mom laugh, even if that laughter was cruel and spiteful, she considered this to be akin to belonging. Even with all of the abuse, even after everything my mom did to her, she still wanted my mother's approval. It's twisted.

I remember this one Christmas—and we even still have pictures of it—my mom dressed Nadine up like a cheap whore, complete with slutty clothes and caked-on makeup, my mother decked her out in a teddy and a feather boa, then she made her get in a box and wrapped her up like a present. During the opening of presents, a large box was given to Kenny, the boyfriend of our rent collector, Darcy, and everyone in the know sat around watching and waiting for the hilarity they knew would come. Sure enough, Kenny went to open his great big present and out pops a sadly provocatively dressed Nadine, clearly enjoying herself in the stripper role as she saw that everyone was laughing and clapping at her performance. Emboldened by what she saw as approval she took her role further and tried to kiss and hug Kenny, gyrating uncomfortably and making everyone laugh. To everyone else there that day—and I should mention children were present during this little Christmas surprise—Nadine was the butt of the biggest joke of the holiday season.

Outside of these rare bits of Nadine's presence for amusement, she was either cleaning the house, being beaten, verbally or sexually assaulted, or in her dark hole of an apartment in the basement doing God knows what. I imagine she prayed down there or maybe she was too exhausted by everything to do it any longer.

Nadine and Luke were both used in other ways as time went on too, ways that were one hell of a lot more dangerous. But to my mom, they were expendable people—as long as whatever happened to them didn't affect their ability to clean or help dad with the apartments, anything was fair game. Nadine was used for just about anything my mom needed done by a middle-aged woman that she didn't want to do herself as well as being a punching bag for lawsuit money.

Back during the Cabbage Patch doll craze (which was a sweeping phenomenon if you remember the moms lining up outside of stores and half beating each other to death over the toys) my mom put Nadine to good use. She lined up with her at one of the stores before the race for Cabbage Patch dolls was on, not giving her any indication about why she was there outside of getting a doll—a fact that Nadine probably pretty readily accepted. As the stampede into the store ensued, my mom seized the moment and pushed Nadine under the feet, causing her to fall directly underfoot during the mad dash inside. My mom stood there and watched—encouraged—as people rushed all around her and then, switching into the role of caring citizen, she howled over the trampled Nadine. According to video and indictments I believe this to be true. Ater that incident, "Nadine" (my mom, actually) sued the store for vast sums of money after this "tragic" event.

Nadine's boyfriend Luke was also used and abused to get money from false lawsuits. I still don't know quite what happened and to what extent it was intended or accidental, but one afternoon my dad and Luke were in the garage working on a truck that was hoisted up. Without warning, the jacks fell and instantly broke Luke's leg in half. Without a moment of thought, my dad quickly hoisted the wailing Luke up under his armpits and dragged him into the middle of the street and left him there, screaming in pain before he finally passed out. Dad didn't intend on Luke getting hit by a car or anything, but he made sure to place Luke in the center of a giant pothole that dad had been after them to fix. When Luke was revived, he was instructed to say he fell in the giant pothole. Luke (my father, as you probably figured) sued the city for thousands of dollars. I don't know if that car was rigged to fall on Luke's leg on purpose or if it was an accident that a second of quick thought turned into a goldmine in the end. It probably doesn't matter, my parents got what they wanted at the expense of someone else.

Not a bad deal for someone else's broken leg and just the minor effort of dragging someone into the street. It was a beautiful thing, having the Carpenters around.

Where There is Loss, There is Always Something to Gain...

Anytime someone lost something of value meant, for my mom anyway, that there was something to be gained. In that way, she was a bit of a twisted optimist—always seeing what could be salvaged from the ruins of people's lives. It always helped when the losses were clean and took care of themselves; in other words, for her to gain something, she wouldn't have to lift a finger to set the wheels in motion.

I was finally past the bed-wetting and daily beating phase of my youth, although that's not to say I didn't get my ass beat still on a semi-regular basis for other things or nothing at all. The addition of Nadine's kids to our family took some of the pressure off of me; she seemed to notice me less, which was a blessing. Lucky for the Carpenter kids, the pressure on them was going to be lifted slightly as fresh meat was brought in once more. This time, however, they were what my dad would call "family" even though Mom wouldn't claim them as her own if her life depended on it.

It was during this approximate time, right around Christmas, that we got a late-night call from the police. My dad's father, who lived with his second (and much younger) wife, Anne, in a six-unit house on Bagley Street, was in the hospital. There had been a large, devastating fire. My grandfather, who I really didn't know well at all since, of course, my dad had to break ties with his family for the most part at my mom's orders, had run in to try to save his wife and their kids. He went back into the fire, but when he opened a door on the second floor, he was caught in the back draft and fell down the stairs, suffering from severe burns. While he tried hard to get everyone out, he was not able to get his wife Anne out. However, my grandfather was still a hero and he was nothing like his son. Nothing like his son in the least. To add to even greater tragedy, a few days later, just after Christmas, he died as well.

Having lost both their mother and father quite unexpectedly, the next several weeks of that year were chaotic and painful for those kids, my father's half-siblings; Freddy, Marie (another Marie—not Nadine's daughter), Katie, and Robert. Although they were closer in age to us kids, the four were my half aunts and uncles since they were my grandfather's kids. Again, they might as well have been strangers to us. We'd only ever heard about what trash they were anyway since that's what my mom thought of any of my dad's family.

All four kids were under 18 when this happened, so of course, that meant the state got involved in the placement efforts. As always, seeing an opportunity, a chance to gain from someone else's brutal loss, my mother quickly volunteered to take the newly orphaned kids under her wing. As you might expect, the same blind agency that had made the mistake before made another one, four of them, actually.

We officially had a full house. Those kids started getting a clue about what kind of person my mom was a few days after the death of their parents. Although I imagine they'd already heard the stories about her.

I remember that my grandpa, being a veteran, had a military funeral and a lot of the expenses were taken care of, which was a relief because the family was poor. My grandpa's wife was far younger than he was and like her husband, didn't have much money to her name. Mom never considered Anne to be a part of the family; to her, Anne was common trash, just as anyone else without money was in her eyes. She hated poor people—whether they were technically family or not.

As my grandfather and Anne's children stood in the room with us on a sad afternoon when we were talking about the upcoming funerals and what to do for Anne's service, my mom said coldly, "I don't care if they bury her in a trash bag, fine with me. I'm glad she melted in that fire. She was a useless, nasty old thing anyway."

The shocked look in the eyes of those kids when she said that, it made me cringe. But already, they were getting the idea that my mom could say whatever in the hell she wanted. It's not like it crossed any of their minds to talk back and to try to defend their dead mother. And it was certainly not the last time my mom would ever openly talk about what a piece of shit she thought their mother was and how she was glad she was dead. The cruelty, especially when she hadn't even been buried yet, was immense. My mom knew she was going to get those kids in her house for good no matter what and wanted to make sure they understood from day one who the boss was. She wanted to test them and see if they'd ever dare say anything back to her, I think. And they didn't. They instinctively knew better.

I remember mom telling me how important it was for me to make sure Freddy, who was closer to my age, stayed happy while the child welfare agency decided what would be best for the children. She had to make damned certain that everything had the gloss of perfection, the bullet-proof look of goodness, or else she wouldn't be able to seize this opportunity for all it was worth. I think that the moment my grandfather died a spark of plan ignited and started blazing out of control in her mind. She was determined to keep those kids and later, it became quite clear just how much she stood to gain.

I kept Freddy happy; I liked him quite a bit, actually. For a while it was me, Ricky, and Freddy—all of us approximate the same age. It was good to have brothers, or at least friends or other kids, who were closer to my age and a little more like I was. Dennis and Raymond were quite a bit older than I was and they were really aggressive and hard to just run around or have any fun with. Us younger boys definitely got in our share of trouble, but we generally didn't just go out and get into fights or steal or anything for kicks on a regular basis like they did.

Things were okay for the kids at first—at least as good as they can get when my mom's in control, but as is her system when someone new enters in the family, it becomes critical for that person to begin breaking all ties with friends and family from their lives before the Burts. This wasn't easy for those kids to do, but there wasn't any choice once they'd been "made official" and permanently installed in our house. They had to completely leave their old friends, their old family, everything. For Freddy's sake, I guess it was good that Ricky and I were around or he would have completely lost it. He didn't exactly start off on the right foot with my mom...

Part of my mom's plan, which probably was first hatched the moment she knew Anne died in a fire in a building she didn't own, was to get some cash out of the deal. The bigger someone's loss, usually the bigger someone's payout was going to be. Robert though, just being a kid with no idea how to straight out lie to authorities the way we'd all been coached to do since the time we were old enough to talk, ruined her chance at big money and he paid for this mistake for the rest of her life in any of his dealings with her.

Mom wanted to sue, saying that the fire had been because of a problem with the building. The fire chief wasn't able to find the exact cause of the fire. This left her with the perfect chance, or so she thought, to get Robert and the other kids to collaborate with her to make it look like something had gone wrong with the building and started the fire. Not knowing any better, little Robert made the greatest mistake of his life and instead of saying what he'd been told to say, he let the investigators know that the night of the fire his parents had been arguing about the electrical cords for the Christmas tree. He said there was something wrong with the extension cords that they were fighting about. Using this information, the investigators had a new angle to examine to determine the cause of the fire and this accidental tip-off led to the ruling that the fire was caused by a faulty, dangerous extension cord and not a problem with the building's electrical system. My mom could have killed Robert for that. The beating he got for it was so bad that it's surprising she didn't kill him.

And now that I think about it, the real irony is that little Robert could never have realized that electrical cords in general were going to become a dark theme in his life in ways he'd never imagined.

See, Robert had this other problem and so he didn't get along with my mom too well because of it either…it was a problem I was very familiar with, unfortunately. Like me, young Robert had a tendency to wet the bed. And as you know, that's probably the worst weakness anyone—at least any boy—could have. While I thought it was awful what happened to me all of those years, what I got paled into comparison to what Robert went through because of his bed-wetting tendencies.

Like me, Robert got the beatings with the electrical cords on a regular basis—even when he didn't pee the bed. I seem to think that his were a little worse, a little more intense than my own, but maybe I only feel that way because I remember looking at him and seeing part of myself in him as he gingerly tried to touch his bloody, blistered back and thighs. God, I felt so sorry for the kid.

Robert's punishment for wetting the bed didn't end at simple lashing with the electrical cords by any means. My mom could see that humiliation for Robert was one of the things that made him feel the most terrible and she exploited this to the maximum. She used to beat the hell out of him with the cords, then when she was done, she would strip him down completely naked, put his pissy underwear on his head, and make him stand in the kitchen—stock still and not allowed to move. Sometimes to make it worse, she would take pictures of him while he suffered through this second phase of his punishment.

Small, shy Robert would have to stand there butt-naked with his urine-stained underwear on his head right there in the middle of what was, at that time, the hub of the house. Everyone hung out in the kitchen and even if no one was around, Marie was always in there—she was as stationary as one of the appliances. And Marie, like the rest of the kids in that house, never did anything but laugh her ass off at Robert as he stood there exposed, shaking, bleeding from his back, buttocks, and the backs of his legs with his underwear on his head like a soggy dunce cap.

I can't count how many mornings breakfast-time meant that we were going to see Robert stock-still in a suspended state of sickening fear and embarrassment. It just became a regular thing. In fact, it's disturbing how many things became normal to us that were so far from the norm in any other family that the Burts will go down in history as one of America's cruelest families.

You know, I should mention too that I was still going to church in secret about this time and when I started to see what was happening to Robert, I got a little afraid that God had taken my word literally to make it stop and had transferred all of my pain and suffering on to this poor kid—almost like God decided that someone was going to have suffer and to Him, it didn't matter as long as someone did. It made me feel so guilty. I couldn't stand it.

All in all though, mom still found ways to make those kids pay off in the end. They weren't any good to her without bringing in a ton of cash, so she had to get creative.

Lucky for mom, Robert fell down in the stairwell at his school. He was always clumsy, falling and bumping into things all the time, a very awkward kid to say the least. Always, unsure of himself and his footing. The school called mom and she took him over the hospital where they performed an x-ray. The doctor looked closely, but didn't see anything wrong, which pissed my mom off because she'd been hoping all along that there'd be some problem with his arm so she could take the school system for all it was worth. You'd better believe she wasn't taking Robert to the doctor to make sure he was okay or anything—the foster and adopted kids rarely got any kind of medical attention unless it was absolutely necessary, but again, we got great care on the state's dime by claiming we were them.

I can only imagine the ride back from the hospital—Robert must have felt so low, but still, he kept insisting that his arm was hurting. My mom ignored him for a long time about this but finally, his arm started to get so bad that he couldn't even bend it at the elbow. Frustrated beyond measure, mom took him back for a second opinion where they did another round of x-rays, only to find that his arm had, in fact, been broken the whole time. His inability to bend it caused calcium buildup, which was making it impossible for him to do anything with the arm at all.

Using the claim that he would have difficulty using his arm for the rest of his life—and he did, indeed, have problems with it—my mom sued the doctor who told her there was nothing wrong. Incredibly, she got ninety thousand dollars out of this. And I say that she got ninety grand out of it—not Robert.

She had used a different attorney for this case. The thing was, the lawyer, who had been her legal counsel for countless other shady deals and acquisitions, actually did try to do the right thing for once. Instead of granting Frances Burt full rights to the ninety thousand, he placed himself as a trustee. Now Robert wasn't completely worthless to her, although she had to get creative in how she got the funds from him. It's a good thing that he had this money behind him because I can almost tell you for certain that if she thought she could have gotten away it, she would have killed him through some kind of "accident" or another. The stakes were too high—by that time, given her reputation, it would have been clear she murdered the kid. She let him live on, waiting for the day when he'd finally turn 18 so she could have what she considered to be rightfully hers.

Therefore, to delve a little more into her extortion of Robert it is interesting that she never considered it stealing. She only had to trick him into giving it to her, which was something that was surprisingly easy. Using the trick she'd been refining since she first started owning apartments, she simply started giving Robert things with the simple, kind request that when he turned 18, he could just go ahead, pay her back, and be on his merry way.

Robert didn't know anything about money, so when mom started selling him things, he agreed to pay whatever she asked. For instance, she was "kind" enough to get him a car for a mere five grand, which at that time, was worth a lot more than it is now. It was a good enough car to a kid who doesn't know any better and only pays attention to how it looks rather than how it runs. But in fact, the car was a piece of shit—it probably hadn't cost her more than two or three hundred bucks and I suppose there's a chance it was stolen and she hadn't paid for it all.

In addition to that five grand for the car, she also told him she'd put him up in an apartment—for a price, of course. And naturally, that apartment was going to need a full suite of furniture for it, not to mention some appliances like a fridge, washer, dryer, microwave—the works. Without ever seeing the money, which probably made it a lot easier for Robert to spend it, he paid for all kinds of things for his new life when he turned 18 and could finally get the hell out of the house where so many of his worst memories lived.

Robert didn't realize it, but pretty much everything he bought from mom was stolen from other apartments and was being sold to him for what was probably a 1,000% markup on what the shit would have cost brand new. He just had no idea. The furniture was crap, the car was crap, the apartment was squalid, and everything had been stolen to maximize the profit margin.

By the time he was eighteen, Robert's money had been used up. Mom had all the paperwork to prove it—neat itemized lists of what he had bought and paid for over the course of time. Out of that ninety grand, mom probably invested (maybe) around a grand in stuff for Robert for a nice neat profit of around $89,000.

In the end, after she'd shown Robert how much he'd spent and he realized he was left with nothing, she kicked him out of the apartment since he didn't have enough to pay rent with, stole back all the already stolen furniture and appliances, and sent Robert packing.

Little goldmine, that kid.

Robert's sister, Katie, also had the potential to be another source of income for mom, but unfortunately, things didn't fall into place quite as easily and in fact, trying to screw Katie over caused a pretty big and highly-publicized problem.

I don't know why these kids seemed so accident prone, but anyway, one slippery winter day a teenaged Katie and my brother Raymond's girlfriend, Trisha, were walking to school together when a car suddenly careened out of control and struck the two girls. They were both injured, Katie complaining of back and neck injuries, and although not bad, there was enough damage to get a hefty settlement out of it. Trisha's mom got her daughter a lawyer and you'd better believe my mom had her lawyer on the case right away too—that was too good to pass up. Trisha was going to be okay, but her teeth were pretty messed up, which meant not only pain and suffering, but the problem of having her teeth fixed and the suffering of her appearances, of course.

For Katie however, when the settlement came, it wasn't in my mom's name—it was in Katie's. By the time the money came through, Katie had long-since had enough of the nightmare Burt family and had run away from home. She wasn't really missed, but mom really needed her back because without Katie's signature, all that money wasn't going to be able to do her any good.

Following a fruitless search for Katie, my mom had to get creative. She was an astoundingly resourceful woman when it came to theft. She had Rachel dye, perm and cut her hair to match Katie's, wear three layers of clothing to look like she had more meat on her bones and coached her over and over as she practiced Katie's signature. Finally, feeling Rachel was sufficiently prepared on how to act and write like Katie, Mom carted her off to the lawyer's office to sign a document that was going to make Mom even richer. However, there was a slight problem.

First of all, Rachel spelled Katie's name wrong. Despite all of her coaching and practicing, this was pretty much a dead giveaway that something was wrong. And furthermore, Katie found out about this check—something she had no idea was supposed to be coming to her, and was, understandably, completely furious. It was really the only thing that made her want to come back to see any of the Burts again and when she did, it was to testify.

This was only discovered years later, in 1993, when the house was raided and it added to the long list of wrongdoing by the Burt's.

GOOD OLD BOYS

We were quite the extended family, all of us kids from different backgrounds thrust together in one house. It was always chaotic, even though some of us banded together more than others. For my own part, I was mostly just the one in the middle—I didn't stand out much. Candace was the only girl, Bruce was always the baby, and my older brothers were a bit out of my age range. Generally, the foster kids didn't count in my mom's assessment of our family, but I did like having a few other kids closer to my age to hang out with sometimes.

I was never very close with my older brothers Dennis and Raymond—it's not just because they were quite a bit older than I was, it's more like they were a lot more wild and aggressive than I think I ever could have been. My dad liked hanging out with them though, especially Dennis. Like his friend Fred, Dennis was unpredictable and savage at heart—you never knew what he might be capable of from one minute to the next. I remember being a much younger kid and watching as dad and Dennis would "bond" over their mutual hatred of animals. Based upon what I recall from seeing this first hand, they both hated cats. Like hated them—they couldn't think of enough cruel things to do them. Aside from the general, more "functional" way to kill them like shooting them or putting poison inside a hot dog, which dad did all the time, they would find other ways—ways that were more entertaining. For instance, one of their favorite little tricks was to tie the tails of two street cats together and fling them in the air and let them scratch each other's eyes out. Once, they managed to get them wrapped up on a clothes wire where the two cats, high up and with instinct taking over, completely freaked out and literally clawed and fought each other to death. Dad and Dennis couldn't have thought of a better amusement on a summer day. On his own time, Dad took one of the cats he found and locked it inside a toolbox without any food or air, just to see how long it would take before it finally died.

Raymond and Dennis fought all the time—and fought dirty and rough, especially Dennis. No one got the better of him. He wasn't afraid of anybody or anything. Even after the cops had carted him off to federal prison for drugs-related charges, he would call the cops who were conducting the raid in 1993 at our house and make threats against the lives of any of them who dared to go into his room. I imagine they probably had a good laugh about that, since he was locked away and they knew it was all empty words, but that just goes to show what kind of a dude he was—he didn't fear anyone, least of all cops. This is also the same guy who, when he got moved from the federal to the state prison, wasn't afraid of the beating the guards were setting him up for, after all, he lifted weights and trained all the time. On the day he arrived at state prison, the guards surrounded him ready to take off his cuffs and arranged to have the other prisoners present, ready to beat the hell out of him. Dennis, an even bigger son of a bitch than he was to begin with, realized what was happened and backed himself into a corner, hunkered down, turned off his mind and laid each one of the prisoners out, one by one, sometimes taking on a couple at a time—breaking jaws on most of them in a matter of minutes. Nobody was going to fuck with Dennis. The guards realized the melee they had created and had to break up the fight, too many of the other prisoners were getting hurt.

Dennis had the same proud, crazy, evil streak my mom did—it's one that took over and said "I am not ever going to let anybody get the better of me in any way and if someone tries, there'll be hell to pay."

Dennis in particular made an ideal son for Frances Burt, that's for sure. They were often partners in crime, but I guess saying "partners" wouldn't be totally correct since she usually ended up seeing most of his gains. Nobody in the world could have messed with Dennis; could have proven him to be a fool. No one, that is, except for my mom.

Dennis had been involved in all kinds of shady shit from the time he was old enough to start running around the streets. Drugs, car theft, beatings—you name it, if it was illegal, you'd better believe Dennis was a part of it. When he was a teenager and my mom's little "business" of stealing from stores was really starting to roll, Dennis got his own little group of thieves together. They'd do a lot of the same type of stuff she'd do at stores, stealing outright, but when they'd get done, they needed somewhere to unload the merchandise. For a long time, my mom was a fence for everything Dennis and his friends took. I don't know who she had selling it for her — the movie showed a black guy, but that's the movies and probably not even close to the reality. My guess is that she was dispersing all of it through the many yard sales around town in addition to some people she might have known.

My mom made a killing off of those yard sales she had going on...She'd unload anything she could get her hands on at them and the list of items usually included all the worldly possessions of at least one or two tenants for each and every sale. It was easy to find reasons to kick people out of apartments and keep all of their shit and over the years, she had it down to a science and knew who had anything of value. Mom kept tabs on that sort of thing. Because unlike her son Dennis, who can best be compared to a "grunt" doing a lot of dirty work — my mom, in her own strange, twisted way, was smart. She was especially smart about her criminal activities because she knew what it meant to be subtle. There was nothing subtle about Dennis though, or Raymond, for that matter. Dennis was like a wild animal, especially if he got cornered. He was crazy.

For instance, once when I was a teenager, not long before we moved out of the house on Spring Street, Dennis got himself in some real trouble because he lost his cool and let the animal side of him take over. He had been out stealing at some store with a couple of his buddies and was walking out when he noticed that a security guard was following them. They all started running and got into the car as fast as they could, slamming the door, all ready to get the hell out of there. Dennis had his window all the way down and just as he'd gone to put the key in, the security guard reached his entire arm into the car, trying to push Dennis back and get the keys out of the ignition. Without a moment of thought, and probably laughing like a maniac if I know anything about him at all, Dennis quickly rolled up the window with the guard's hand stuck in it.

I imagine the guard, as he left his hand there, still in a desperate, heroic grasp for the keys, partially thought that there was no way this kid was actually going to roll the window up on his hand or arm. No one would be that crazy—but Dennis was that crazy and he sped through the parking lot with the security guard dangling from the car by his now mangled hand for quite a ways before he finally fell off. Dennis and his friends really hauled ass once the guard finally fell off the car and they hightailed it instantly back to our house so my mom could give him directions on what to do next.

In a frantic explanation, Dennis gave my mom a hurried lowdown on what had just happened. She told him to hurry up and hide and that she'd give him an alibi. The cops obviously knew where to go because it didn't take too long until they were at our house, guns drawn in full raid mode. They went through almost every inch of the house looking for Dennis, who was safely hidden inside a panel in the wall in our downstairs hallway—perfectly able to see and hear everything that was happening but still hidden from view and impossible to detect. They had all of us kids who were downstairs line up against a wall as they searched and yes, it was a little scary.

Now, here's the thing. It was true that the police did have their guns drawn. And yes, I suppose it's also true that it was scary for any kid. But my mom, when she presented her case about the police's behavior and got a huge settlement from the city of Pawtucket, really played it up and made it far, far worse than it was. It was easier to convince the court too with some pretty willing testimonials from the poor "traumatized" children of the house too.

You see, the moment the police left after their unsuccessful search for Dennis I watched as my mom's eyes clicked into that cat-like reflex mode. She became calm, serene, and ordered us all into the camper where we were promptly taken to Butler Hospital. Just before we left, and of course the whole way there, we were carefully instructed to talk about how we had been damaged, psychologically speaking, by the harsh intrusion of the police and the affects of having guns drawn on us.

Of course, based upon the symptoms that we were instructed to talk about, I was placed on a medication for depression called Elavil, which my mom would actually make me take even though I didn't need it. I think she ended up doing this to us because it made us all easier to control if we were drugged. When I took these pills, they would make me drowsy; so tired it would be hard for me to function. There was one time where I know that this almost killed me. My mom forced me to take these pills for years and one summer I was driving back from the summer house and started to fall asleep at the wheel, I ended up getting in an accident and was injured so badly that I almost died. However, at least my mom had her control.

At that time when my mother started getting all of us on pills, after the police incident with Dennis, Bruce was having some kind of issue (pre-existing, of course) with his ability to swallow, which my mom sort of "post-dated" to make it seem as though it was caused by the trauma of having him dragged out the bathtub naked—something that never happened, but of course, as my mom's saying goes, "The law isn't about what's fair, it's about who is the best liar." There was nothing the police could say or do. They had been accused of pulling some scrawny little kid naked out of a tub and now he couldn't swallow due to "nerves." There was just no way of disproving it even though every single one of them knew damn well none of it happened the way my mom or us kids said it did.

The lawsuit against the city was a sickeningly big one. She dramatized it better than any Oscar-winning screenwriter could have, presenting us kids as being so mentally scarred from the whole affair when in fact, we just went back to our lives as usual for the most part. The only difference was, in order to keep up with the claim, we all had to go to these sessions at the hospital to talk about how traumatized we were—those were a bunch of bullshit and went on for what seemed like years—all for a big chunk of money we never saw.

When Freddy finally got the nerve to leave the house and then got caught for dealing drugs, he made an agreement with the police to sign an affidavit stating that our family made the whole thing up but still, the money had been granted and not much came out of the whole denial of what was so clearly the truth—that the Burts had once again royally fucked someone (or in this case, something—the city) over. In truth though, the Burt that did the screwing over was just my mom and accordingly, she was the only one who a saw a single dime from the thousands the city plunked over, supposedly for our care after our trauma.

Dennis eventually turned himself in and got a slap on the wrist for the whole affair. I imagine that the security guard got a nice settlement himself out of the whole deal but probably was never able to use that hand the right way again.

In a lot of ways, Dennis was like my mom—there was something about him, some vital element that makes us human, that allows us to empathize with others—that was just plain missing in him. Like mom, he lacked feeling; he was more animal than man sometimes and was damn scary to be around. Out of all the people who I knew growing up, friend or family, he was probably the one who was the most out of control and brutal—with the exception of my mom, of course. He wouldn't care who he fucked up if he was in a rage.

There's this memory I have that I feel so conflicted about that makes explaining it difficult. On the one hand, it's hard to think about objectively because I was so grateful to have a brother like Dennis, one who wouldn't let anyone step all over me. However, having that same brother who would bash the brains in on anyone even remotely involved in a trespass against me makes the whole thing an uncomfortable topic in a lot of ways.

I was probably around twelve or so when this happened and it really started off as a pretty minor thing as far as incentives to violence goes. My parents had this tenant on Lyon Street, which wasn't far from our house on Spring Street, who had this guy, John, coming around who everyone made fun of because he had a ridiculous nickname. This guy was a pain in the ass and liked to mess with people, I think just to see how far he could push them. He started calling me names, one thing led to another, and all of a sudden, this guy hauls off and slaps me in the face. It was a shock to me. No one had ever done that to me before, except for my parents. Not knowing what else to do, I started to cry a little and went to my dad to let him know about it.

My dad seemed pretty irritated about the whole affair when I told him and he called up Dennis, who was, at times like this, what I can only equate to a Doberman trained to respond to a call—he was ready on the word. Dad swung by the house, picked up Raymond and Dennis and asked me where these guys were—this tenant and his friend.

The tenant was scared shitless when he saw dad with his two big, notoriously crazy sons in tow and directed dad to go down to the basketball court, where this John was supposedly hanging out. Dad drove down to the schoolyard and when I pointed the kid out, they all jumped out—all at once, and surrounded this John. Part of me started to feel sorry for him.

They didn't just gang up on John. They started beating the hell out of anybody and everybody who was there in that schoolyard. At some point, Dennis must have decided the whole thing was taking too long, so to expedite the process, he ran to the truck and brought out a hammer. He made quick work of every person out there, it didn't matter who they were, how old they were, or if they just happened to be bystanders— he just bashed heads with the hammer left and right. I will never forget that metallic, hollow "pop" as people's skulls split open like fat, split grapes. The blood was everywhere; it was like someone had turned on a fountain of it and let it spew everywhere.

That was just the kind of crazy family I had. I did, however, watch what I said about anyone who might have offended me. I didn't mind taking care of things myself and will never forget that sinking notion of knowing how many people probably suffered brain damage that day simply because some idiot happened to slap me.

The moral of the story: you just didn't mess with my brothers. Or my dad, for that matter. Especially if you were some low -life renter. Because my parents were landlords and when you hear someone talk about how bad their past landlords were, I can almost guarantee you they had nothing on my family.

Another memory I have is where I would go out with my dad to collect rent—he was always in a dark, jolly mood on those days and oftentimes, we'd all come along with him, although God knows why he would want us along. After all, my dad had been in deep shit in his life as a landlord for trying to exchange sex for rent on multiple occasions—not sure why he'd want a bunch of kids tagging along.

So there we were; it was me, Freddy, and Ricky sitting on the back bed of my dad's pickup truck waiting for him to finish, not really concerned with anything that was going on. The building we were parked outside of was basically like two houses, each of which had six families in it. It was a summer day and we were glad to be out of the house, even if we were over at some crappy building with our dad. There was plenty to see since the weather was nice, everyone who lived there was outside in front of the house. The kids were playing and the adults were chatting away as the evening approached.

We started to notice that the easy chatter was giving way to raised voices. I remember that the tenants were starting to band together a little—it was looking like a coup was about to take place. They were all talking to dad, some of them with louder voices than others, talking about the big problem with cockroaches and rats. There was a heavy moment of silence before they broke the news—they weren't paying their rent until the rats and roaches were gone. Period.

With my family as the landlords, you don't say you're not paying your rent. That just was never an option. If you had rats or bugs, in my mom's mind especially, it was your problem— you were just trash anyway. This one guy started threatening my father when he told them their rent needed to be paid. And the threats started getting more intense. The argument got heated and my dad immediately got on the phone with Dennis, who was at a friend's house, and told him to get his ass out there—there was a situation. In the meantime, dad jumped in the car with the tenant in hot pursuit and we started to take off, all of us kids still in the bed of the truck, exposed to the evening air and this lunatic who was chasing after my dad, making every motion that he was going to ram our legs with his car. It was scary as hell but we made it back to the house in one piece and scrambled inside, knowing we could have gotten maimed or worse.

However, the call that my dad made turned the tables. Dennis and seven or eight of his buddies went out to that building where the tenants were refusing to pay their rent and took care of things. They jumped out of the car with clubs, chains, and bats and beat the living shit out of everybody who was out there. This means everybody. Not just the dads but the moms, and not just the parents, but the kids too. A couple of six year-olds got the hell beaten out of them by Dennis and his gang— anyone old enough to possibly even try to fight alongside their parents got beaten.

About an hour and a half later we heard Dennis and his friends outside of the gate. He was furiously honking his horn and I noted that all of the guys in the truck had red faces and their eyes were wide, shining, angry. They pulled into the yard and quickly filtered into the house after shutting the gate tightly after them.

Sure enough, not long after the cops surrounded our house and were asking for Dennis to come out. Of course, Mom lied and said they weren't there.

Would you believe it, this was another time out of countless others that the Burt family never suffered any consequences. Because nothing...nothing at all, ever came of it.

ONE OF "THOSE BURT KIDS"

We had achieved a level of infamy in our own community and pretty much anywhere else we went. With my fearless brothers and the mass of the rest of us—all kids who, in one way or another, had been through one hell of a lot in our short lifetimes, we were usually a force to be contended with. And we did, I am ashamed to admit, get in our share of trouble. Unlike other kids though, normal kids from normal, stable families, we rarely suffered consequences for our actions because more often than not, my mom stood to gain from the trouble we got into. The only time we got punished was when we'd do something that would cost her money.

Dad showed us boys how to make Molotov cocktails, bombs made of gasoline-filled bottles with rags inside that could be thrown and burn just about anything they came into contact with. It was also around this time that I learned how to make guns from scratch, which was something that I thought was pretty neat as a kid. Of course, looking back now I see how dangerous it was, working with the matches and flint that we'd break apart and crush down into a fine powder, not to mention the lighters. That stuff was, after all, the best substitute for actual gunpowder—the same ultra-combustible stuff that could be used to launch cannons in the old days.

We'd work hard grinding away at the matches and flint, then we'd take the powder mixture, break off a piece of metal from a bike spoke, and turn the spoke into a gun with a handle. We'd mash the mixture into the spoke, just like the cannons from the old days that used gunpowder, then take another spoke, cut it into a small piece and put it in the barrel and heat it with a lighter until the metal would ignite and explode, scattering hot pieces of metal everywhere. And I do mean everywhere. After all, we used to do this in the house all the time. We'd hold contests inside with this stuff—once we had an explosion that sent a piece of metal a full half-inch into a solid wood door.

I have a scar on my arm to remind me of another time when we were playing around inside with our homemade guns. Dennis rigged one of his creations up for me and the barrel blew apart and went into my arm—a long piece of hot metal, right into my arm! The pain was unbearable but my mom, who never winced at anything, just walked right over, pulled it out, and sent me on my way. Dennis was eventually indicted and prosecuted for the crimes he committed that destroyed property.

In my house, there was plenty of yelling, screaming, and fighting, but we never got yelled or beaten for doing shit like nearly blowing our hands or arms off with improvised explosives in the house. Now, if we messed up and got the family in legal trouble or blew a cover, you'd better believe we'd get our asses reamed. But with regard to ordinary things (for our family) like firing homemade guns in the house—not a single word.

As kids, we had a real way of lighting things up and gradually, as we got older and a little more innovative, we moved away from simple handmade guns that didn't do much outside of give us a thrill and began experimenting with "pineapples" which were illegal fireworks that were roughly equal to about one-quarter of a stick of dynamite.

The pineapples alone were fun, but soon we started to think up ways we might be able to put them to use and, unfortunately for a lot of people, we did find a way. What we'd do is take that pineapple, which actually looked like a small stick of dynamite, and we'd light a cigarette, measure it onto the wick and then wire-tie the lit smoke to the wick. Then we'd stick this under the windshield of a car—right under the hood—so when the wind blew it would make the cigarette start to burn slowly down. The wick would eventually blow up. Once the wick blew, the hood of the car would be completely destroyed and the windows inside the car would all shatter. It was a sight to see—we would run as far away as we possibly could the moment we tucked the nasty lit surprise under the wiper blades, making it someone else's problem.

Over the course of my youth, I don't know how many cars we annihilated with the pineapple bombs, but it's a number I certainly wouldn't be proud to admit to. Our destructive little invention led to a lot of property damage, especially in the little town where the summer house was.

I remember this one guy who used to run a motel near the summer house. Behind his house there were all kinds of perfect sand dunes that were great for dirt biking on. Well, the guy wasn't thrilled about us riding on his property and like pretty much everyone else who lived around us at the summer place, he hated our family. He was always calling the police on us but it would always take the cops a long time to get over to his place and by the time they did, we would be long gone. It used to piss us off that he wouldn't let us ride back there and we went complaining to mom about it.

Most "normal" mothers would probably give their kids a stern lecture about respecting other people's property or would ground them for getting the police called in. Not my mom. Her response to our complaints was, "Well, if he's pissing you off, you know what to do…," and that would be the end of it. She was pretty much giving us free license to get revenge on the guy, which we certainly did. In one short evening, two well-placed pineapple bombs did their duty and completely destroyed both the motel owner's car and his wife's vehicle—just for good measure.

Because we were the Burt kids, we did it; it was what we knew. Because we were protected by our mother — at least in the legal sense — we always got away with it. There was probably never any kind of question about who the guilty party was for the cops in that town when people's boats — people who, for whatever reason, had the nerve to piss off our family during our summer stay — were blown to bits.

Dad was one of the most creative when it came to getting loot out of the area's residents who summered near us. My dad used to get scuba gear just to dive underwater, swim right underneath people's boats, and steal boat parts as well as anything else he could find. I can't say that was anything I ever wanted to do, and besides, we had our fill with all of the other opportunities for procurement that lay in wait during the summer. Dad was never prosecuted for this, as they had so much on him, it was just another crime he got away with.

The Summer House

Even though we got in one hell of a lot of trouble at the summer house, it is the one location that holds some pretty decent memories for me, but mostly just because it was a break from the sad routine of abuse that was going on at the Spring Street house. When we were at the summer house, we ran free — we were unhindered — it was a license to escape the everyday struggles of our lives.

When I mention the "summer house" I am referring to one that we built — not really the one that stood when my mom first bought the place off of some lady. The woman she purchased it from knew the beauty of the house and I think she was more than a little sad to see it go. It was old and had been the source of summer fun for several generations before we got our hands on it, I imagine from the high wooden vaulted ceilings, the rough varnish of the sea-beaten knotty exterior, and the homey, salty smell that wafted in and mixed with the forest scents through the open windows at night, I was in love with the place. It was such a gorgeous house, at least in my eyes.

My mom hated that house. She had it in her head that it looked like an old, dumpy cabin. Frankly any house that might have anything that could be called "charm" repelled her. She liked new things—shiny things, and the old, beautiful knotty pine of the house that sat on the property irritated her, spoke of something that looked "trashy" to her. And truth be told, the only reason she bought the house was because it sat on a large double-lot. In other words, she didn't buy the house for the house, she bought it for the land. Because as always, she had a plan—probably from the moment she first laid her beady little eyes on the place. The plan, of course, involved a fire.

Of course my mother was subsequently charged for these crimes eventually in court. The summer that she bought it, I had the hardest time figuring out why in the hell we had to take all of the nice, neat furniture out of it and transport it back to our house. It seemed to fit so well with the feel of the whole place—but this was what we were told to do, so we did. We spent a couple of days heaving the heavy wooden furniture out and replacing it with a bunch of junk stuff that had been removed from old apartments. Most of the appliances we put in there didn't work. We also had to bring any clothes that we had there back with us—basically anything of any value. In its place—in all the places in the house where stuff should have been, different, but older and much junkier stuff was put in the place of the things that actually had value. When we were done with the our little "refurnishing" effort, the house was filled with just about every piece of non-functional, stolen, and otherwise undesirable thing my mom could find. Even the drawers in the bedrooms were filled to the brim with old, often stained and torn clothing. To anyone walking through the grand old place, it would appear that dirty bums had taken over.

And then, the summer house—that regal, rustic place I was

so excited to explore summer after summer—suddenly, inexplicably caught fire. With the old pine and years of coatings of varnish, it all but disintegrated in no time flat...nothing was left of it.

My mom was delighted. It didn't take long for my teenaged brain to register what had happened and why we had been asked to take out anything of value and replace it with junk. After all, it would have been too obvious that she was committing insurance fraud if the house was miraculously empty when it "mysteriously" burned.

I have no idea what ridiculous sum she received for the house itself, but she got close to ninety thousand dollars for the contents of the house alone. She left no stone unturned during that tallying process—socks, shirts, toaster ovens, picture frames—she factored everything she possibly could into that grand total for the insurance company to pay back. While all of our real stuff was safe and protected back on the home front, the only stuff that burned in the fire was total trash anyway. I don't think any of us had ever owned a single thing that burned in that fire.

And what a great start for her to build her house on that double-sized lot she so loved! Unable to sacrifice all of her profit on that fire, she pocketed a lot of the money. Instead of trying to outdo the neighbors or rebuild with a vision, she made use of the charred lot by bringing in a bland, characterless modular home—one that contrasted sickly with the other homes in the community that had weathered the years in their towering, hardwood glory. To her, at least it was new and was cheap. Screw what anyone else would think—it was her land, her place.

And what was more, she had a whole summer of free labor to help her get it done since all of us kids—and by that time there was a boatload of us—were off of school and at her command. We all had a real investment in that place because when you got right down to it, we're the ones who did all the work inside to make it as nice as it could be. We even helped furnish it...

You see, even with the huge settlement from the fire, my mom wasn't about to spend any money if she didn't have to, especially on a bunch of smaller necessities like cookware and other things that we would never use when we were back at home. For those things—camping gear, cookware, you name it—we were sent out during the heat of the day to raid the nearby campgrounds, which had been abandoned for the afternoon by campers who sought relief from the heat at the beach. It was ridiculous how trusting people were at these campsites; like they never realized that people like the Burts really existed. It was like stealing candy from babies as we made around the campgrounds and the outdoor patios and other areas where the summer folks from the town entertained. It only took a couple of nights out hunting for supplies, to return with plenty of pots and pans to serve at both houses if necessary and tons of other great stuff for summer fun—toys, outdoor games, balls, bikes— you name it.

Another nasty thing we did one time at the summer house was steal a jet ski from a neighbor who left it sitting overnight in the water. While this was a typical practice and was done by many of the residents of the community because they didn't expect another neighbor to steal, they clearly didn't understand how the Burts operated.

Late one night, we swam out to where our neighbor had their jet ski sitting, unprotected, in the water. We didn't start it, but just slowly, quietly pushed it along over the water until we made it to our side of the lake. We weren't stupid enough to ride around on it or anything the next day; what we did was load it up in secret onto a truck, take it back to town with us, sell it, and then use the money from the stolen, older jet ski to buy a nice new one.

Another time at the summer house, we were driving around and noticed this house, all isolated and away from the road that looked abandoned. After casing it for a while, we eventually went up to it, just out of curiosity. Inside, the place was fully stocked—just as if someone had been there somewhat recently but left in a hurry. We kept an eye on it for a while, always taking a few things here and there when we'd stop by, and no matter when we went, it was like no one ever lived there. One day we got fed up with just taking a few things at a time and just brought a truck with us. In the span of a short few hours, we stole damn near everything in that house and left it bare. We never did find out anything about it or hear about it— it was like this place that lay in wait, just for us.

And you're wondering; what did people think about all kinds of stuff going missing as soon as the Burts moved to town? Didn't they start to suspect something?

Well, hell yes, they suspected something. They knew it was us. But we'd been raised to believe—trained to believe—that it didn't mean shit who knew or didn't know something was true or that you were guilty of something. The only thing that mattered was whether or not they could prove it to the authorities. If they couldn't, then nothing else meant anything. You got what you wanted and they got screwed. It was just the way it was.

And people around there—all of those blue-blooded New Englanders--oh my God, how they hated us. Mom had some rowdy, loud parties out there during the summer with all sorts of people that a lot of the uppity people turned their noses up at. It was loud some nights, but after a while, the neighbors closest to us learned that they'd be best off if they kept their mouths shut about it. One couple, who was always calling the police on us, learned the hard way when all of their nice, expensive patio furniture was at the bottom of the lake the morning after a complaint. Over time, people did just sort of back away and refuse, as much as possible, to acknowledge we were among them.

We did a lot of pretty terrible stuff during the crazy summers of my youth. I recognize that now and believe me, even then I knew, very clearly, the difference between right and wrong. When you're in a family though, that not only encourages this sort of thing but expects it, it's damn near impossible to back out of anything. Like any other kid, especially one who was kind of lost in the shuffle, I just wanted to fit in. I wanted to be a part of the family—one of the gang. And in the Burt family, being a part of the family meant doing the things that the family enjoyed or found to be useful or beneficial somehow. The problem was, of course, what my parents, especially my mom, considered good was usually illegal or otherwise just plain wrong. We were, after all, just kids.

LOVE SAVES THE DAY

As a teenager growing up in the Burt family, there wasn't much to look forward to—I got my kicks where I could, but I didn't really have a place that I fit into that I felt comfortable being in. At school, I did a pretty half-assed job. My parents really didn't care about school or the homework that any of the kids would bring home and I remember report cards being a non-event in the household. Where most parents would scrutinize the report card and reward or punish accordingly, my mother would sign off on them without looking at them. She simply didn't care. The only advice we ever received regarding our behavior at school was one that said, "Act up, don't take shit from anyone, especially your teachers." She didn't care if we got suspended or sent home for bad behavior. The way she saw it was if we weren't at school, we could be working at the apartments or doing other forms of her bidding. School detracted from her personal goals.

At home, I wanted to nothing more than to escape and go somewhere else, somewhere that was normal. My mother encouraged us to be shameless opportunists and to take care of people who would either stand in the way or had the potential to become a problem. And when I was with my brothers, I usually just got in some kind of trouble, often the scary sort of trouble—people getting beaten up, stuff getting lifted from stores. I just felt like I was wandering, floating, waiting for something to happen.

And then, something did happen. I met Arlean, my wife—she was a shy, beautiful girl that was a little afraid of me at first. She only knew me as a kid from the neighborhood and we weren't introduced until after about two months of her living in the area. She might have heard about the reputation my family had in our community, but never could I have dreamed of what was going to befall her by getting involved with someone like me. The woman who stuck with me from the time I was a teenager and struggling with my family, all the way until now, years after that family who tormented the both of us for so many years has dissolved. My wife of many years, a woman that children call "mom" and others call "grandma." There is a song that I have always associated with Arlean and with our relationship, it's called "I Love You," by the Climax Blues Band. I have always felt that song was written especially for us.

If you'd ask her, she'd say that she'd do it all again—put herself through the suffering and nightmares of becoming part of my family—but if she said she wouldn't, not even for me, I wouldn't be able to hold it against her. I couldn't blame her. Being strong-willed meant that my mother had a natural aversion to her and from the time she started coming around until long after it was clear that she was going to be with me forever, my mother made it clear exactly how much she hated her.

The first time Arlean caught sight of me I was walking out of the middle school during the middle of the afternoon when the "good" kids—kids like her, were supposed to be sitting in their classes, paying attention, making the grade, and doing all the things normal kids probably did. I was leaving because I was supposed to go to the principal's office for a detention, but I hated detention and just decided to walk out. The only reason

I was in school anyway was because I loved my industrial arts class, otherwise, I really could have done without the rest of it. At that point, the school was getting fed up with me and was starting to tell me I couldn't go to my industrial arts classes— needless to say, that first time she saw me I was in a pretty terrible mood. Still, something about me stood out to her, made her look twice.

Later that same week, a friend of mine who also knew Arlean introduced us. We all went together to a baseball game and from that day on, we started dating. Unfortunately, just as we'd settled into a good friendship and relationship, Mom decided she was packing all of us up and we were moving to Cumberland, which would put a little distance between us. Still, we spent all of our time together, listening to records, hiding from the world—there was nothing that could separate us then and, for that matter, even still today, regardless of some of the bad decisions that I had made that inevitably put her in precarious situations. Regardless of some of the regrets I have, she still was able to fall in love with me. Believe me though, there were some serious wedges driven between us from those first times of being together all the way until we were living together with our children.

You see, I think I've mentioned this before, but if there was one thing my mom couldn't stand, it was someone, especially a young girl out of all people, who would dare tell her "no" or refuse to go along with her plans. Arlean came from a good family with strong values and for her, the way our family was run was nothing short of shocking. From the beginning of our relationship and especially as time wore on, my mom tried everything to split us apart, including lining up woman after woman to try to seduce me. She hated Arlean, but Arlean was okay with that fact because she hated my mom too. She knew what kind of twisted woman she was, but she loved me and was determined to stand by my side through anything. And she did—she stood with me through more shit than any wife should ever be asked to. That is true love; when you are willing to sacrifice yourself for the sake of the one you adore.

The sacrifices that Arlean had to make for me fill me with the greatest love I've ever known, but they also fill me with a certain kind of sadness. I am sorry that she had to endure so much hardship simply because it was me she decided to love. Why she didn't just find someone who came from a nice, happy, normal family—someone who could have given her a stable, enjoyable (but also maybe sometimes boring) life—is beyond me.

From the minute she started coming around, Arlean's life started getting more and more complicated. She'd never met people like us before and soon, as my family made up their mind that they didn't like her, I started having to make some sacrifices too. This one night, Arlean and I were sitting on the couch, settling in to watch a movie when all of a sudden, my brother Dennis and his friend Bob sauntered in. Seeing Arlean and knowing how pissed off it would get me, Bob casually sat down, almost on top of Arlean, and put his arm over her, pulling her close. He looked me straight in the eyes and said, "Hey Randy, see this? I'm gonna take your girl," and held Arlean close to him. I knew that look in his eyes—Bob seemed to always wear that expression that said, "And what you gonna do about it?" but I couldn't take it. Without a moment of thought, I summoned up all of my strength, routed it to my arm, and punched Bob directly in the face as hard as I could. And I could tell that even Mr. Tough Guy was hurt—bad. He didn't do anything to me at first, but Dennis went and told Dad. And when Dad came rumbling in, you'd better believe there'd be hell to pay. He told Arlean to get out of our house and as soon as she'd run out the door, very upset and unsure of what to do, he beat the living shit out of me. And that wasn't the only time I got my ass beat simply for seeing Arlean. But still, somehow we made it work. It became all about sacrifice, even from those first days of our relationship as teenagers.

Arlean had infinite patience with me. It's like she knew that many of things about my life that she hated—the crime, the trouble—weren't really part of who I was deep down. She knew I'd been raised to accept the unacceptable. In the end, she saved my life; probably more times than I could ever know or count. Still, even after we met, I did some things that I am not proud of. As her control over me began to exert itself though, I came to rely on her advice, to listen to her, to let her help me live a better life, even when everyone I was surrounded by was happy to let me just eek out an existence and stay a slave to my mother's whims.

Growing up in the kinds of neighborhoods we did and being the type of people we were, you'd better believe that we were a little rough around the edges. I think that this is part of what Arlean noticed about me first; something about that made me attractive to her. I wonder too sometimes if it was the element of danger that I posed to her. After all, she was a good student from a nice family—she had everything going for her and usually walked the line. She needed something to spice up her life. God knows she found it.

And when Arlean found me, I don't mean this in the typical sense of "finding" another person who you fall in love with. I really mean this in the way people talk about being "found" in the spiritual sense. Like that song, *Amazing Grace*..."I once was lost, but now am found"...You see, I feel that way because time and time again, Arlean ended up saving my life. She just seemed to have a sixth sense about when I should or shouldn't do things, who or I should or shouldn't be around. While she didn't know all the details, she had a feeling that my family was involved in a lot of shady stuff and with a lot of less than reputable people. She knew she couldn't stop me, especially since I faced beatings if I didn't follow suit with my mom's plans, but she always seemed to know when and how to protect me. She could see from the beginning that my mother wanted to use her as a tool, trying to use her to make me do things.

I will never forget the night she saved my life—the night that if she hadn't said something, hadn't tried to keep me just a little longer in her comfortable presence, I would have either been dead at fifteen or in juvenile hall for one hell of a long time on some serious assault charges. A huge fight occurred at one of my mom's houses and had I been there, my future would have been incredibly different. Thankfully, I had been with Arlean.

I don't want to make it seem like my family was the only screwed-up or violent group of people in our area or anything, but I will say that we were quite a presence, especially my older brothers—Dennis in particular. With some of the people we had for tenants though, my mom was probably thankful each and every day that at least one of her sons was a completely insane son of a bitch who wouldn't think twice about completely destroying someone's world over one little slight. With this in mind, you'd better believe that by the time I became an adult, I had seen more than my share of violence—not just within my own family, but in the neighborhoods I grew up in.

This is one event that will never leave my mind—it took place at one of my dad's properties on Rhode Island Avenue. It was one of the tenement buildings that seemed to plague damn near every street, which were interesting places because so many different types of people were all jammed right on top and next to one another—a recipe for drama, for sure. Anyway, at this particular property there was a group of local bikers that everyone knew as the Freedom Gang. They were notoriously loud, obnoxious, and were, most of them anyway, just as insane and aggressive as my brother Dennis.

When my brother Raymond and his girlfriend Trisha found out they were going to have a baby, mom decided to move them into that building and recruited me, Freddy, Ricky, Dennis and his friend Bob to go help them get moved in. We were supposed to arrive around 7 p.m. on that hot summer night and I distinctly remember Arlean holding me back, telling me she didn't want me to go. I wanted nothing more than to stay there with her at her house but still, since it was already 7:30 and I was already late, I knew I would get my ass kicked if I didn't get in gear—I reluctantly hopped on my bike and rode over to the property. On my way there though, I stopped by own my own house and noticed that the place was empty, except, of course, for Marie who never left the kitchen unless something major happened. But this night, something big had gone down.

"Didn't you hear about what happened?" asked Marie, her eyes wide with a mingled look of excitement and fear. "There was some huge fight down there where everyone's moving on Rhode Island Avenue. Really bad!" She seemed surprised that I didn't know about it and just as I was getting ready to get back on my bike and rush over to see what had gone down, Dennis stumbles in, shaking with anger and covered in blood from his head to his shoes.

He looked quickly from me to Marie, "Are the cops here yet?" he asked. We shook our heads and dazedly, but as if someone had lit a fire under him, rushed up the stairs and showered.

By the time he came back down, we were really wondering what happened. Once Dennis was sure the cops weren't there, he explained to us what had occurred. According to my brother's recount, apparently, the group of bikers started antagonizing Dennis and Raymond for some reason, probably just because they were drunk and bored and not expecting for anything to actually come of it. Little did they know they were messing with Dennis, who didn't care if he was facing an army of armed men—if he was pissed off, he'd take out anybody, or at least try.

After some words, the bikers jumped the fence and an all-out brawl ensued. Dennis fought one after the other and luckily for him, most of them were drunk, otherwise with that many he probably would have been dead. Dennis explained an excited and detailed blow-by-blow recount of the fight, "Yeah, so one guy came running at me—he kept getting back up. Finally, I just grabbed his arm and I put it on the curb, you know, like held it down real strong, and I bent it back and it just snapped like a twig. I could have torn the motherfucker's arm right off if I wanted to!" He was laughing, still bleeding, and still shaking with excitement about the whole thing—my brother really got off on stuff like this. He said the only reason he hadn't ripped the appendage off at the shoulder was because the cops were starting to arrive and he decided to get the hell out of there. Besides, he knew that the cops would take care of everything.

You see, in my neighborhood, the cops weren't what you'd call loyal protectorates of the peace or even equal opportunity defenders. They'd all had their share of run-ins with the Freedom Gang, as well as the Burt Family. The cops hated us both, so instead of jumping in to break up the fight, the cops saw their golden opportunity and whipped out their billyclubs and starting wailing on everyone, most of them who had already fallen due to the liberal ass-whipping Dennis, Raymond, and Bob doled out. They took full advantage and just laid them out cold, one after another, adding to their injuries. The cops probably figured it was about time they got to do this, issue a liberal ass whooping and be able to blame it on the members from either party, walking away scot-free.

It was a total bloodbath—one of historic proportions. They beat the hell out of them, handcuffed them, and while their arms were behind their backs, they beat them some more. The cops knew that with a fight that big, no one was going to be able to tell what happened when; for all the public would know, those guys were beaten within an inch of their lives by the assailants—two of which were my brothers.

Dennis and Raymond won the fight but they definitely had to pay—both of them were charged with felonious assault with a deadly weapon since at some point, they both managed to get their hands on baseball bats. It ended up costing my mother close to $12,000 to pay for their defense in court. They lost—

and you'd better believe they both had to find a way to pay her back.

All I know for sure is that Arlean knew that I couldn't leave her that night. I fought to go simply because I knew my ass would be done for if I showed up any later than I was already going to be, but I remember the earnest way she pleaded with me to just stay there—that for whatever reason she just knew that she did not want me to leave. I owe that woman my life in more ways than one and for countless more reasons than this one instance. Still, it was uncanny how she had a knack for keeping me out of trouble. She had never wanted any part of anything that had to do with my family. She never was interested in their ill-gotten gains, the properties they owned, or their way of manipulating others to line their own pockets. She was only ever interested in me.

If I had shown up at Rhode Island Avenue, there would have been no choice but to throw myself into the fight. In my family, especially where my brothers were concerned, you did not back out; you did not get scared and run. You stood your ground, especially if your family was there with you. If I had shown up and tried to weasel my out of that fight, I would have paid for it for the rest of my life through ridicule, physical abuse, and God knows what other kind of hell. Leaving was not option—not for the long-term and not for short-term but devastating things like bloody, savage fights with biker gangs. With that said, if I didn't end up getting killed or maimed in the fight, my best outcome would have been being convicted of assault with a deadly weapon. I would have been handed a bat and I would have been expected to use it. Period. There were no other options.

It drove Arlean crazy that my brothers got in so much trouble—that I was constantly in danger. But she is an angel. Without her, God only knows what would have become of me. But I was not perfect; too many negative things had been drilled into me for too long.

With Arlean's arrival, into my life came a lot of changes, most for the better, some for the worse. I can't lie—I made some really stupid-ass decisions when I was a teenager and while they started to taper off as Arlean's influence grew on me, I am guilty of doing some things I regret. I think that part of the reason why I always felt that keen sense of the angel on one shoulder (Arlean) and the devil on the other (my family—and especially my mom) is because I was still trying to figure out who I was and who I wanted to be. The good part of me, which was a part that was far more powerful than anyone, particularly in my family, cared to see, desperately wanted to live a content, peaceful life without crime or drama, just simplicity and happiness. The other part of me, however, no matter how small it was in comparison to the positives, was brought out by negative influences without much trouble. My family was the greatest negative influence in my life.

Unfortunately, even with Arlean around, there were times where the trouble I got in, was really hard to get out of. There was a woman who lived across the street, she was an old retired school teacher and was probably on the verge of Alzheimer's. I was around sixteen at the time and had taken to hanging out with Arlean's brother on and off. He had been able to get her to agree to pay him $100 just for sweeping her sidewalk and when my mother heard about this payout, she encouraged me to go see if I could get anything out of her.

Now when I say that this lady had lost her mind and probably shouldn't have been in control of any money, I mean it. We pulled a lot of shit on her. After I introduced myself, I reported back to my mom and we started to scheme. This woman was so senile that we were able to tell her there was a little boy who lived upstairs who snuck in her house all the time and caused trouble when she wasn't looking. We said this boy was tipping over furniture and damaging her house and needed to be taken care of so he couldn't hurt her property any longer. Of course, we offered to take care of him for her—this phantom boy in her attic causing trouble. "He's really big," we told her, trying not to laugh. "We need a grand to get him out; a thousand dollars each. It's a really tough job, lady, and we're taking a big risk going up there all by ourselves to capture him and get rid of him for you." We told her we saw him sneak in all the time, it became a running joke for us and a running story for her—she wanted to know about this bad little boy causing trouble. We just really couldn't believe how gullible the lady was to believe such a thing was happening; I think at that point it was mostly just funny to us...sure, we thought about actually taking her money to get rid of a problem that we invented, but when my mom got wind of the boy in the attic story, she about shit a brick, "What do you mean you haven't charged her for getting rid of him yet? Are you boys retarded? Get your asses over there and charge her to get rid of that boy!" We told her finally that if she paid the little boy in the attic $2500 he would leave. Of course, she paid.

The whole thing was so ridiculous in its own right—that here is this lady who seems to have access to a money tree or something and is already more than willing to pay us about 500 times over what normal work would cost and now she'd pay us more than we could make in a year at a regular teenager's job to get rid of a problem that only existed in our imaginations? But Mom pushed us and pushed us harder. She also made it clear that we were to get into that house and find all the gold, silver, and jewelry and to bring her anything that looked like it might have a chance of being valuable. You see, when my mom sees something like this that's too easy to pass up, it doesn't matter who stands to lose—even if it's a mentally ill, lonely elderly woman—she is going to milk it for all it's worth.

Another time we made up a story that a building inspector was coming around and that her house needed new paint to pass inspection. We told her we would be willing to do this for her, for the price of seven grand. However, this is where I messed up.

All of the money that this woman was taking out of the bank was enough to start drawing some serious attention from the people in charge. We were probably being a little too greedy from the very beginning, but I think we could have managed just fine on the "small" chunks of change we were getting. My mom's incessant pushing to get more and more though is what I think really drew attention to the matter. The bank started to see these constant withdraw amounts in cash that were high enough to raise some eyebrows and they finally just flat-out asked her what she was doing with her money. She probably very innocently told them about the nice young men doing work for her, painting her house, and getting rid of the obnoxious little boy in her attic and they, in turn, probably rolled their eyes and took some action. The radar was on. The bank manager nodded his head and asked her to bring one of us in the next time we needed money for a job around her house, you know, to sign for a check. So one afternoon when we were asking her for another several thousand dollars to paint the other side of the house, she showed us her empty hands and said, "Oh, it looks like I don't have any cash on me, boys. Let me go on down to the bank and get you your money. I really want you to come with me." Not thinking a thing was off, I went.

When we got to the bank I was met at the counter by the manager, he asked me to sign for the certified funds, which I did, signing my name without a second thought.

I never would have thought the old lady had it in her to pull anything on me — a Burt, but she did.

The bank looked at me like a criminal from the moment I walked in, but I still didn't think too much of it. They asked me for ID, asked me some questions, and then, instead of giving the old lady a wad of cash, they gave me a certified check in my name.

By that time, I had a hefty sum accumulated from my work with this old lady. Of course, even though it was my "own" money, mom kept it for me and bought me a car — a beautiful

Mercury Lynx that made me feel like the world's biggest badass. There seemed to be no limits, no end in sight to my new source of income until a day about a week after the check was given to me at bank. The police called and asked for my parents. I had to go downtown where I found the lady from the bank sitting there, looking at me through narrowed eyes. "That's him, all right," she said, looking at me like she could have killed me if they'd let her. That day was kind of a sick blur—a court date was set and worse yet, even worse than the fact that I knew my income was gone and I'd be reduced to whatever kind of menial job I'd have to find after that, was the beating I knew was on the way. Sure enough, when he got home, we marched right on over to that drawer—a drawer that I had stopped seeing as regularly as I did when I was a kid—and she beat the living hell out of me with that electrical cord, almost like she was making up for lost time.

In the end I stole just about twenty-one thousand dollars from that woman, which I had to pay back. See, but here's the really screwed-up thing about that beating. I wasn't getting the shit beat out of me because I'd done something awful and cruel like steal money from a helpless old lady—God no, that couldn't be the reason, especially since mom would have done it herself and probably done it better if she knew of a way into the old woman's trust. No—I was getting my ass beat because I accepted a check and stole the wrong way. I was, in other words, being punished for getting caught, not for committing a crime.

I plead "not guilty" to the crime, but that didn't work for me that time, even with my family's clout and probably especially because of their reputation. I'm sure that judge already knew both of my older brothers by that time and now, here I was, another Burt doing something against the law. I was ordered to pay the old lady for what we stole over the course of just a couple of months. Furthermore, I got locked up for the first time in juvenile hall, which was probably one of the worst experiences of my life. I sat in there for one hell of a long time before mom finally gave up fighting for my innocence and paid the money to get me out. On top of bailing me out of juvie, mom also had to fork over the full $21,000. You know though, if she hadn't done that, I would have had to sit there in juvenile hall until I was twenty-one years old or until mom was able to pay the restitution. I was lucky to only have spent two weeks in there, but that was enough for me. Mom had the money, of course, but she didn't want to pay it. That money she paid, I should mention came from the huge chunk of cash from the city that was awarded after the motor fell on Luke's leg—oops, I mean, from when Luke fell in the pothole. With so many lies about what "really" happened, it gets hard to keep the facts straight.

Another thing that I remember my mom telling me with a certain reverence in her voice during this time; "Remember, when you go into court, keep in mind it's not about the truth. It's about who can lie better. Whoever's the better liar will win—don't you ever forget that." In this respect, I think my mom is right. Every court case I was ever in, it all came down to lying, both parties involved. My mother had the tenacity of a high-level lawyer, whenever one of us had to go to court, she would coach us for hours and hours, drilling us on possible questions that could be asked and what our response would be. She wanted to make damn sure that we wouldn't mess up on the stand and this became common practice in our house. If she wasn't such a criminal, she would have made an excellent lawyer.

This whole situation in my life did indeed complicate things with me and Arlean. I was on my mom's shit-list in a pretty serious way and I owed for my mistake. On top of that, the fact that my parents hated Arlean and thought she was a goody-goody was complicating matters even more. They weren't sure how to proceed and knew that nothing was going to stop me from seeing her, despite their best efforts.

At one point during all of this, I tried to run away. Arlean and I devised a plan for me to stay at her house until we decided my next move. One day, I snuck out and left Cumberland, making my way to Pawtucket, where Arlean lived with her parents. While I traveled, my absence had been noted and Raymond made it to Arlean's house faster than me, threatening her parents with not only a beating, but stating he would set their house on fire if they attempted to house me. When I got there, I learned about what had transpired and realized I had no choice. I returned to my family's home, with much chagrin, because I couldn't stomach the idea of anything happening to Arlean or her parents, just because of me. They were too good to put at risk.

However, this experience also ended in the fact that it was becoming clear to my parents that they couldn't beat Arlean out of me, so I think that in some way, they let it be for a while, at least until they figured something out. It was obvious that nothing they could do or say was going to make me let go of her. Her parents, for their part, knew what kind of family mine was and they were kind—they understood what I was coming from and were welcoming, good people, making sure I felt better than I ever could when I was at home, whenever I was around. It was actually always sort of strange being over at Arlean's because her family was actually friendly, they seemed to genuinely care about people, including, of course, their daughter.

As if on cue, it must have occurred to my mother that if she couldn't figure out a way to separate me from Arlean, she would come up with a way to get her closer and benefit through the manipulation of my girlfriend.

One day, my mother decided that she didn't want me going back and forth between Cumberland and Pawtucket to see Arlean, as it took me away from the "family business." She, quite calmly, suggested that it would be in everyone's best interest, at least hers that is, if I got Arlean pregnant.

While this seems like the opposite of what any responsible parent would be telling their teenage son, you're right. However, responsibility was the last thing my mother had on her mind and of course, her own selfish interest was behind this new plan.

My mother figured that if she could make Arlean part of the family by getting her to pump out some kids, she could ultimately control her, and me. Mom tried to keep her outright expressions of hatred for Arlean at bay for a while she pushed her plan on us pretty hard within the first year we were together. Eventually, because things like this happen, she got her wish.

Of course we weren't married at that point, but when Randy Jr. was born, my mom had exactly what she wanted—control over our lives. As much as Arlean and I wanted to get married, that was strictly prohibited. My mom absolutely refused to allow any of her sons to get married. Sure, we could be in a monogamous, long-term relationship with kids, a house, and all the other normal trappings of marriage, but the institution itself was forbidden. This applied to Raymond and his girlfriend of many, many years, Trisha and of course, it also applied to us. She didn't allow marriage because if Trisha or Arlean decided to divorce one of us, we would be stuck paying child support and it infuriated her to no end to think that we'd be paying for our kids while our wives were shacking up with someone else. She had a low opinion of women in general and considered those who were members of her gender as whores, looking to get whatever they could out of a man. I suppose it's natural she'd think that since that was the way she was.

To get Arlean and I, as well as keep us under her thumb, she offered to let us live in a house directly behind hers in Cumberland with our new baby. We were just glad to be together and have a place of our own at first, but by that time, my mom's noose of power was wrapped tightly around Arlean's neck. Just before she got pregnant, my mom was already working on her to get her to stop talking to her parents altogether. And slowly, it began to work.

You have to understand, that one of the biggest threats to

the power that my mother was able to exercise was that of external influences. When someone became a part of the "family," she wanted that person to relinquish their contact with the outside world and those people most important to them.

Now that she was giving us a house, filled with furnishings, and was around us all the time, there was no way to resist her—my mom forced her (and when my mom forces, believe me, there aren't loopholes or way around things) to cease all contact with her family from that point on. Without a choice, Arlean became a Burt.

Now another thing, as Burt family sons, we were not allowed to do was be on our children's birth certificates because again, this might make us financially responsible if we split up with our children's mother—and what a terrible thing that would be in her eyes, the responsibility for our children, not splitting up with the person we love. Essentially, I had to "adopt" my own kids later in life. However, this setback to my future translated to something more important for my mother. This meant that with no marriage or birth certificates for the children stating that I was the father, my mom was eligible to file for welfare and any other state aid she could get because in their eyes, the woman in question was a single mother. And I say that my mom was eligible for Arlean's benefits because as you probably guessed, that's just about what it came down to. My mother would get the "wives" to file for welfare and turn over their checks to her, allowing them only to have the bare minimums. My mom took most of what Arlean got every month. After all, she'd been so kind as to provide us with a nice house and kindness *always* has to be repaid. I should mention that Arlean always hated the idea, but she was a teenage mother and needed a place to live—we both did. We became victims of circumstance and my mom's trickery, just like everyone else in the family at one time or another. At one point, Arlean was after me to just leave, move out, leave our future to chance, but at least try to live our lives for ourselves. However, my mother got wind of it before we could hatch our escape plan and instead decided to reel us in farther, building us a new house and filling it with furniture. This was something we couldn't do on our own, and our plans for escape fizzled. Eventually, we had our other son, Michael, not too long after Randy Jr. and you'd better believe that made Frances Burt a happy grandma—not because of some overwhelming love for her family and grandchildren, but of course, because more children meant one thing—more checks.

According to the charges filed, we weren't the only ones being manipulated and used at the hands of my mother.

Trisha and Raymond had the same thing going on with the state aid, which was actually a pretty hefty sum each month between the food stamps and checks. Mom was also getting a boatload of money every month for the other foster kids, as well as from Nadine and Luke's welfare and Social Security checks. Everyone around her turned out to be a bigger goldmine than she ever could thought possible while also functioning as what amounted to servants to her. It was at this point in time that her shoplifting plans started getting even more in-depth and involved.

And so life went on for us. Not the life we'd planned on having by any means, but a life nonetheless. When the raid came and ended everything, Arlean and Trisha were both charged with welfare fraud because of all the money they'd "earned" over the years. However, I helped get Arlean's charges dismissed. I testified that she had been forced to commit this fraud by my family, specifically my mother. But in turn, I took responsibility for the charges so she could emerge from the entire fiasco without a felony in her past. I really didn't want her to carry a criminal record because of her history with me. Over the course of the hearing before a Grand Jury, the judge and jury got an idea of the magnitude of my mother's control over all of us and this did help things. These are all things I'll talk more about later, but it's worth mentioning now because it was such a big, heart-wrenching, guilt-inducing part of our young lives.

And to jump ahead once more, let me tell you, the first thing we did when we were finally free, once the raid happened and when my mother had been put away and we started to see light in the darkness of our lives again—we went right out and made it official; we got married. I was so proud to call Arlean my wife, officially. It was the first big decision I had ever made entirely on my own, and I knew for sure it was the right one.

PART II
Twisteo Systems

The Family Business

I am the black sheep of my family now and I am quite happy about that. However, one of the things that my family is best known for, unfortunately, is the way we conspired to steal so much (and in so many diverse, creative ways) from stores in our area that we literally put several out of business. I don't know how many hundreds of thousands of dollars we stole over time by switching tags, messing with the barcodes, filing false returns on stolen merchandise which we then turned around and used to get even more—I just know it is a significant amount of money.

I suppose that with that in mind, I should make an important distinction. When I say that "we" conspired, it is true. All of us were involved; from the oldest to the youngest and everyone in between and even outside the family. Everyone who was close in some way or another with my parents was part of the operation, which spanned over the course of many years. It began around the time I met Arlean, but by the time I had turned eighteen it was a full-scale effort. The thing is, the "we" behind everything we did was my mother. She was the ringleader, the coach, the instigator—the creator of what ended up being one of the most notorious theft rings that ever operated in the region's history.

The coaching started young and none of us were free from it. If one of the kids (or grandkids—she did this with my own sons) were too young to actually do any stealing, they would be used as little storage devices for stolen goods. I am telling this incident only to recount what happened, I encourage no one to attempt these criminal acts and I can assure you it would not work in today's technologically advanced world. I remember, for instance, when my parents took one of my kids to Florida to hit the Disney theme park. You'd better believe they came back with a boatload of gifts and souvenirs, none of which they paid for. It was so easy to steal with kids around, I am horrified to think about how they used their own grandchildren. "I love that hat on you!" she'd drawl, using her best cute little grandma voice. "Go show your grandpa! He'll love it!" and then, she'd keep the clerks distracted while my little one came tottering out of the store with a nice new hat that just happened never to get returned to the store. That was how it was—nothing and no one was sacred.

There should be no mistake in what had happened with the family business—although we all had a role to play in the shop-lifting scheme, it wasn't because we were thrilled about doing it. It was the way things were; it was part of what we were expected to do. What a lot of people don't understand was that in the Burt family, you didn't have a choice. You were either in or you were out—and if you were unlucky enough to be out, you could expect that your life was going to be taking a drastic turn for the worse in just about every way possible. We were all at our mother's mercy when it came to getting by and we did what she said. She knew that she had us wrapped around her finger, so with the fear in place, all that was left for her to do was to coach us into becoming the best thieves we could be.

In addition to showing all of the kids and later, their wives, how to shoplift, she would always be in the background providing instructions about what to do in any situation and furthermore, the best way to steal so that we could get the most out of a store. For the girls, there was an easy way to do this; she had an elaborate plan that worked several times. The idea was hers and worked because of her persistent, relentless coaching.

She would instruct all of the girls, if they got caught, to deny everything, even if it looked like they'd been busted red-handed. If there were no cameras, they had free reign according to my mom's preaching about the issue. They had to make themselves appear that no matter what, they were not guilty of stealing. With the denial in place came the important step—and my mom explained this to them very thoroughly. They were to make sure there were no cameras, then they had to rip their shirts and scratch themselves to the point of bloodletting so they could say (and show evidence) that the security guard tried to search them against their will and exposed and fondled them in the process.

This little plan worked marvelously. For instance, at this one store called Jumbo's, (which eventually changed it name in an effort to save itself because we were hitting it so hard), a department store that was like Target, Rachel, Candace, Trisha, and my mom got caught stealing. Following my mom's instructions, Candace tore her shirt at the top and scratched her face and chest, leaving big welts and red marks all over, like she'd just been in a struggle. She told the police that the security guard took her to the back and wanted to make sure she didn't have anything in her bra and that he groped her—none of which was true. She also said she didn't have anything and did nothing wrong—not true either. She had been switching tickets and the cops did end up arresting her. However, when the case went to court it ended up getting dismissed because of the tussle that supposedly took place and nothing came of it. That was immediately followed by a large civil suit against the store because of the sexual assault that Candace had claimed. And guess what? Like usual, the Burts won the case—although I should make it clear that in reality, my mom won the case. Her expert coaching made this pay off big time and accordingly, she raked in the settlement. There were many, many civil suits like this filed by members of the Burt family. Whether it was slip and fall, insurance fraud, sexual assault, negligence, on paper, we looked like one very unfortunate (and well compensated) family.

Another thing we would do on my mom's advice was bait the store detectives into making a false arrest. It didn't take us long to identify exactly who the detectives were. We would get them following us around the store after clearly taking something and hiding it so they saw us do it. To them, we'd been just as good as caught. We would then lose them for just a quick moment—long enough only to discretely put whatever we'd taken away. Then, after we'd get to the door, they'd say, "you need to come with me" and we'd put up the innocent front. They'd watch us the whole time, then the cops would come to frisk us, only to find nothing at all. Believe it or not, we would end up getting $15,000 to $25,000 for this sort of thing in a typical civil suit. We didn't like doing it, but if they were watching us we knew we wouldn't be able to steal due to security anyway, so this was as good way to make our little shopping trip worth it in the end.

My mom would teach us that we could take anyone for anything, it didn't matter what it was, as long as we were confident when we delivered our scam. The most important lesson in my mother's repertoire, was the importance of presentation. That was the key to everything and was the reason why we got away with as much as we did over the years. She drilled the idea into us that there was great importance in keeping up the act—of putting on the show and being about as two-faced as any person could possibly be. We would hold doors open for people, always be polite, well-mannered and nicely dressed. We never, any of us, looked punky or trashy or like the sort of people who do something as drastic and wrong as we did for so many years. Out of all the coaching and brainwashing we went through, it all boiled down to presentation. How to make yourself totally believable as the one telling the truth even if all you had to say amounted to one lie on top of another.

Presentation and confidence were the key to everything that qualified her as one of the most manipulative women to ever walk the face of the earth. Presentation alone was the key to her ability to steal a child from its mother. Presentation was key in somehow, even after allegations of the worst kinds of abuses, getting more and more children to foster and hanging on to those who clearly shouldn't have been in the house. Presentation was the key to every form of fraud; insurance, tax, you name it. She was, to put it mildly, a skilled faker—an imposter. A wolf in sheep's clothing.

Daily Operations

Switching price tags sounds like the easiest thing in the world to a lot of people, but it was surprisingly difficult and stores were always trying to find new ways to change their system and make it harder. In the beginning though, it wasn't so bad once you got used to it and knew what you were doing. With the old school price guns, clerks would just take a gun, set it with the SKU number, and then stamp it on the item. There was really nothing complex about it for them and for us, it was like stealing candy from a baby. All you had to do was find something from the same department, peel the little sticker off, put it on something far more expensive, and the rest would be history. I can't count how many times we used that tactic. We'd find something easy that we wanted, for instance, a shiny new KitchenAid mixer that retailed for $300. With our eye on that item, we'd walk around and look until we found another mixer, but of a far cheaper brand. You wouldn't believe the price variances that came into play for what amounted to just about the same product. We'd often find the same type of item (in this case two mixers) but with a price difference of a few hundred dollars. Back in those "good" old days, all that was involved was a quick peel and replace, and bam!—we'd be paying $29.99, which was the cost of the super-cheap mixer for a product that sold on the upwards of $300.

With that part finished, all that was left was the selection of the perfect cashier for ringing up our purchase. The young girls were always the best—bored high school students with their head in the clouds and no real firm idea of what things were supposed to cost. You could get almost anything through on these types and over time, we became experts in judging cashiers. We were really never wrong either—they would be so trained to look at the tag and while they might notice that yes, it was all from the same department, it never occurred to them that the item they were totaling up was far more expensive than the one we were technically paying for. It was gloriously easy back in those days. As we grew more experienced, we'd have our ideal cashier picked out as soon as we walked in the store with one quick glance. There was nothing to it.

When you left things to my mom, nothing was ever "enough" when it came to getting things for nothing. She was greedy and her system fed on this—this character flaw made us boatloads of money over the years. You see, once we'd paid for the much cheaper item, the major part had only just begun. We weren't just interested in getting nice things for cheap prices— we were out for pure profit. Naturally, this meant that somehow we'd have to get money in exchange for our nice, high-end items. This is where the price switching system really kicked in.

Once we'd checked out, we'd head out to the car and switch places with each other. Usually, after one of us kids—and we had been so carefully coached that there was hardly a chance of anything going wrong—came back out, mom would go back inside. She was by far the best. She would take the original price tag with the SKU on it for the expensive product it was, then go back to get store credit that would be applied to a new product. Then, she would get another product with the store credit, grab a receipt for a product that we paid cash for, switch the tags, and voila, we had a profit!

Eventually stores just started getting smart all-around and made the switch to electronic barcodes. However, switching barcodes worked the same as switching price stickers, it didn't stump us or stop us. All we had to do was sit there, and it was time consuming indeed, and dissect packages by shifting barcodes. This is where my real place in the family business started to come through. I wasn't mean or cruel like Dennis or good at switching tickets, but Mom realized I had a knack for technology and so I came up with a way to switch barcodes from one package to another even if it was imprinted on the box.

I am about to reveal something that no one knows about; this is the first time I've ever come clean on this—they did find pricing guns at mom's house but this information was never released by the police. The only thing in the reports was that we were switching price tickets. However, that stopped in the early 1980s because of barcodes so the police and the courts missed out on a whole new and bigger level of criminal activity.

We did a good job of figuring out some things about barcodes though; we were nothing if not industrious. We started to understand that there were no specifics on barcodes. So, to make an example, if you were to take a box of Legos— something that was expensive but easy to do this sort of thing with, especially if you got the kind of Legos that come with motors and other small, expensive parts, you'd see that that box was worth around $200. From there we would get another, smaller and less expensive box of Legos, something in the $29 range that would have the same size barcode on the back.

I would buy the cheap one, take it home, and with the utmost care, I would take a sharp razor knife and lightly slice around the code by sliding the knife just under the paper. If I did it correctly it would all come off in one neat piece. Just before going into the store to return the item, I would then get a high quality glue stick to make sure it could be applied evenly and smoothly, turn the code upside down, rub it with glue, and get it all ready to go in the palm of my hand where it was hidden from view. All that I had to do from there is lightly stick it on—which is something that took practice to be able to do it smoothly, and simply paste the barcode over the other one, making sure to get all the bubbles out.

This wasn't always as an exact of a science as I would wish, but over time and with some practice at home before this event went "live" it worked quite well. At this point in time, barcodes were no longer a total barrier for the Burt family and this new system took off. Of course, there were a few rules we had to follow, just like any other time we did something like this. For instance, we had to make sure the cashier was as out of it as possible, especially with something like this that carried a little more risk than our old system of switching tags. After all, there was always a chance that even the most careful placement could go wrong or the glue would decide to give up.

It was almost flawless though. After I became an expert at it, you had to look really closely at a barcode to even come close to seeing that anything was amiss. The key was to make sure the cashier didn't look closely—distracting them with conversation or idle talk was always good—anything to keep them from paying attention before they stuck it in the bag without a single clue what kind of mistake had been made.

This got even more interesting as time goes on because before too long, all of the kids were part of this, as well as Nadine, Luke, Trisha, Arlean—it was a massive shoplifting scheme. And it paid off like crazy; there was no stopping us. Not only were we so good at it that no one ever suspected a thing, but there were just so many of us involved that there was no way for the security teams at the stores—all of whom absolutely knew that there was a big theft problem even if they weren't sure how things were being lifted—to keep track. There was a such an organized system of who would steal what, who would take it in and return it, who would use the store credit that it would have been impossible for them to know how they were losing so much money without some specialized surveillance. We were robbing these stores blind and they couldn't figure out how we were doing it.

Furthermore, Christmas was entirely another story. Just as most families spend more during this special time of year, the Burt family, conversely, stole more. Christmas was the most intense; mom bought us a van and a camper just before the holiday season one year just for this purpose. We would all pile up together, have a discussion in order to lay out the plan for the day and decide who'd do what, and then we'd be off, "making" what amounted to many thousands of dollars in a single day.

It was ridiculous and we had it down to such a science that we evaded detection until some stores were put right out of business. And that's not just me thinking that we had a bigger effect than we did. We literally put places right the hell out of operation—the Burts alone closed their doors and unfortunately for them, none of them were the wiser.

If you want to see my family as a cult—its own sick religion—then no other time of year could have been a more decadent celebration of all of our "glorious" wrongs than Christmas. If an outsider were to have walked into one of our Christmas parties, they probably wouldn't be able to believe it. It would seem like they had walked right into a royal party for some noble family. After all, down to the red carpet, my mom gave every appearance of us being royalty.

As the foster kids got older, our Christmas celebrations got bigger and bigger, as they were able to do more for my mother. Therefore, we were more organized and the "hauls" got bigger. Christmas presents eventually were stacked to the ceiling, filling an entire room. From "small" gifts like high-end watches, jewelry, and electronics to big things like massive televisions, motorcycles, dirt bikes and everything in between, Christmas was complete mayhem. On a typical holiday, walking into the room where the presents were, you would be looking at thousands upon thousands of dollars in merchandise. And yes, you guessed it, if it's wasn't stolen straight-out, then of course the money used to buy it was the direct result of our work.

I suppose it's natural to see how Christmas then would become another extension of this kind of madness. My mother had the holiday spirit, all right. She'd go all out, just this one time per year, for people in and outside of our family. And what this did, especially for the outsiders, was keep them hooked. Yes, Frances Burt was a conniving, evil woman who everyone knew would fuck them over for a nickel without a second thought, but they all were strung along by her parties and her presents.

The gifts were big and expensive, the parties, particularly on New Year's Eve, were enormous—everyone wanted to be there in her basement. But in the end, when the holidays wound down and my mom knew that what she'd given to them had them all where she wanted them—in her debt, whether they knew it or not. It was then that she'd go right back to the way she was with everyone. It was this way from the time I was little until Arlean and I were adults struggling along without stealing and trying to get her presents that she would be happy with. It was hard for us to live without being criminals, especially when it came to making her happy. One time we gave her an inexpensive Tiffany lamp and she got angry. In turn, she took back all of the gifts that she had given to Arlean and I and our kids and kicked us out of the house. Merry Christmas, right?

Sometimes, when I think back to all of the people who the Burt family harmed, I think about all of the retailers we put right out of business. All those people who lost everything; their jobs, their dreams of having a successful business, all of their hopes for having a great Christmas themselves. Then I remember the ridiculously overstuffed room full of presents, each and every one of which were the product of someone's broken dreams. When I think about this, I am sad beyond words. But back then, especially when I was younger, it was just a natural thing. We just felt lucky not to be getting our asses beat on that one day of the year that she was too busy to bother noticing us and to get a bunch of gifts. But we did work hard for those presents—from the youngest to the oldest, everyone was part of that nasty business that allowed us crazy, over-the-top Christmases like that.

However, Christmas wasn't the only time for giving gifts in my family—if my mom liked you, of course. My youngest brother, Bruce, was the one who got birthday parties. He was the one who got the closest thing to genuine affection that my mom had it in her to give away, although that still meant plenty of hatred and abuse. But he was the one who got a big birthday gift and it was enough to make us all a little jealous. All it cost was one's man ability to ever work in his field again, to ever shake a felony conviction, to ever be able to clear his name of a crime he didn't commit.

When my brother Bruce turned sixteen and wanted a car, my mom told him, "Take your brother up to the dealership and have him pick out a car. I don't have time to waste car shopping—you guys just pick out what you want and let me know."

With a statement so generous, even if it was something related to her dear little baby Bruce—a kid who was allowed to get away with far more than any of us ever did and who was much more cruel to Marie and the others than any of us could have dreamed of—we knew something had to be fishy. But off we went to the dealership; what fun was that to be told to go and pick out any car anyway?

So we were there for a couple of hours before we finally settled on the right one: it was a brand new 1989 Firebird with only 20,000 miles on it, and Bruce was in love with it. We told the guy at the lot we'd be back with mom and settle the whole deal then. Bruce could not believe his luck and that dealership had no idea what it was in for.

A word of warning to car dealerships about this next story, it is not my intention to give an instruction manual on how to steal a car from your company. I encourage no one to try this, you are not likely to get away with this criminal act. My mom was a shameless haggler. When it came to anything she'd have to pay cash for, it was never beyond her to struggle and fight with the seller to get as much as possible for as little as possible. She'd already agreed to put five grand down and after her remarkable haggling efforts, she talked the guy down to $19,000 for the car. He was okay with this and set about drafting the paperwork, reminding her that as long as she does agree to put that five thousand down in cash on the spot, they have a deal.

So my mom is sitting there, digging through her bag like's she's some absent-minded person, making sure not to stand out or be suspicious in any way and finally she emerges with a large stack of cash. She counts it out right in front of the guy's eyes and you know he's thinking, "What a deal—cash down payment and another car sold, good for me." My mom puts the large stack of cash on the desk casually, all the while keeping him busy with questions, distractions—putting him completely at ease and making sure the nature of the conversation is light-hearted and amicable.

She chats away, turning on the charm while he gets the dealer plate tags and other ownership information together. Offhand, she says, "Oh, and what I need too, just so I don't forget, is a receipt if that's no trouble." Without a thought and with the gleaming pile of cash right there in front of his eyes on the table, he does so gladly—writing out a careful receipt with the $5,000 down payment all nice and accounted for. With that receipt, he also puts the key to the car on the table with professional ceremony. The car is hers, after all, that deposit is sitting right there and all the paperwork appears in order outside of a few little signatures he needs from his superiors.

The guy, still laughing after something mom's said, tells her to hold on a second while he runs out of the room for a quick moment to get some things signed by his boss. She smiles politely, tells him it's no problem, to take his time, she's in no hurry. He returned and my mother persisted with the questions and then began to take interest in another car. The salesman of course, went into full on sales mode, especially since the paperwork and deposit were all wrapped up with the first car. However, in the midst of all of it, and after asking the salesman to take her out to the lot to show her another car, my mother slipped the money, the keys to the new car, and all of the appropriate paperwork in her purse.

Of course, they went out to the lot and my mother didn't buy that other car she was feigning interest in. She left, with the money and full documentation that the car was hers and the deposit was paid. The salesman, probably disappointed he wasn't able to close the nice lady on car number two, went back to his office. However, there was something missing, the five grand that had been on his desk. He probably didn't even suspect her at first. He probably wondered if he hadn't put it in a drawer for safe-keeping. But no—he knew he hadn't. And the only option was the worst possible one. Had that sweet lady actually stolen her money back and ran? And oh my God, he had written her a receipt and everything, hadn't he? And yes, he thought to himself…he gave her the key, too. All of this probably occurred to him slowly before it started to roll in his mind and he realized that the worst was true. And he was screwed.

By the time mom got home with Bruce's shiny new car, the phone was ringing. The dealership wanted to know, "Had she maybe just accidentally not paid the man?" or "Did she happen to just accidentally take that money that was sitting there, at least according to the salesman?" The boss of the dealership was the one calling because needless to say, by the end of the day, that salesman was in jail for theft. He would have lost his job, his life, maybe even his family, because of what my mother did.

But my mom didn't think in these terms. That's what he deserved for being a retard—a total sucker. Bruce's Firebird turned out to be a pretty cheap car in the end.

A Formal Education

It wasn't until I was an older teen that I started to find my place in the family. Dennis was the brawn, Raymond was the conniver, and I happened to enjoy the technical side of our family business. So it was a natural fit for me to enroll in college in East Providence at a technical school where I could study computer programming. I did this not because I was hoping to become some kind of office man working on developing programs or software—I did this so that I would be able to anticipate and alter existing and new barcode scanning technology. I needed to have a full understanding of how barcodes worked and it was at this technical school that I was able to learn this and a lot of other useful things.

As far as education goes, I didn't have a lot of positive influences. I did have a high school diploma, thanks to my industrial arts teacher, who wishes to remain unnamed. He was the type of teacher that when I quit school became upset because for so many years, he had been the one person who would always be in my corner. He wanted to see me graduate and go on to do great things. He was my mentor and was a positive influence in my life, one of the few. I considered him a "Big Brother" figure and thankfully he took a liking to me. While it is true that my mother had him fooled, he knew there was something going on, he knew something was wrong, but wasn't sure what.

I enjoyed the time I spent with him, because it came with none of the stress I felt when I was around my house. He used to take me from my house and out sailing with his family. While we were out he used to make me read books, which I always did, even if it wasn't something I wanted to do. He was a person, one of the only few in my life at the time, who encouraged me. He knew I liked sailing and said if I didn't read I couldn't sail. It was during this time that he started to encourage me to get my GED. It was that simple. At the end of the summer the time came for me to get myself back on track. He said I was all set. He picked me up and took me to CCRI to take my GED, waiting until I was done. He was there with me to hear the good news that I had passed.

As my industrial arts teacher and mentor outside of school, he also taught me all about construction. When Arlean and I were given our first house, there was no deck on it, so he ended up coming over and assisted in the building. He didn't necessarily build it for me, instead making it into what resembled a class project; how and why—not just making me his right hand, but teaching.

Because of all that he did for me, he became my oldest son's godfather. He was probably only twenty-eight when I met him, and he still lived with his mom and dad when he was helping me out, but I remember just how nice they all were. They were some of the only people I knew who would treat you well just because they wanted to—not because they were looking to take something away. In my house, there was no "niceness" just for its own sake.

Regardless of my teacher's help, I know I disappointed him. After everything happened he felt betrayed and I just let things go. I remember trying to call him a year after the raid and when he answered he was polite, but I knew from the tone of his voice that everything, including our relationship, had changed. There was a "hurry up and get off the phone" tone about his voice and it hurt. If I could say anything through this book, it's that I'm sorry for the pain I caused.

I have a thousand regrets about things I've done but when I

get right down to it, one of the worst is that I disappointed him the way I did. I found out some time ago that both of his kind, old parents died and I didn't have anywhere to send flowers or my good wishes. My heart aches when I look back on this situation—I feel that if he had been my father, I would have really been able to accomplish something great. He saw the potential that was locked away inside me, and while he tried his damndest to unlock that door so I could explore my possibilities, that box was sealed so tight after years of abuse and being told that I was a nobody. If only it had opened, between the positive influences of Arlean and my teacher coupled together, I might have gone far.

A Profitable System is Not Always a Perfect System

While we had the shoplifting thing down pat, sometimes we did get caught. My mom got busted at a place that was like Best Buy in those days. She was in the store and had Trisha, Candace and Arlean with her. She was switching tickets and sent Arlean to the register with an item. When she finished, two security guards got Arlean and brought her to the office and handcuffed her. They had mom on the camera switching tickets and handing items to Trisha. They ended up getting Trisha in handcuffs, and got ready to go after my mother, who was walking out without paying, rounding everyone up. The police came to the store and took them all downtown. My father ended up having to go down there to pick up my mom and Trisha, but Arlean who was a minor, couldn't get out without calling her parents. However, my dad certainly didn't want to involve Arlean's real parents in what had been happening. That would have been enough to bring some heat down on my parents. So, they decided to have Nadine go down to the station and act as Arlean's mother in order to spring her from jail. The cops never stopped her, but they knew that Nadine was not Arlean's mother, in fact, I am convinced they let her go because they felt sorry for her, or maybe for both of them.

Furthermore, even when my mom got caught at something red-handed, she would always fight it. She would insist she wasn't guilty; stating "I'm not guilty" like she believed it herself. Mom got caught another time, but this time it was just she and her friend ChiChi from Panama—she was having Chichi put meat in her pocketbook at a grocery store. The police spotted them doing this and arrested both of them at the register. Of course, the two of them were freaking out because they wanted to find a way to beat it and this was only possible because there were no cameras.

I came up with the idea to help mom and ChiChi beat their charge; they had to send somebody in to fill out a job applications, putting the date she got caught and the time on the application so they could say that it was a guy filling out an application who saw it happening. This person would say it didn't happen and would be a witness! The lawyer could check this out and he wouldn't know "the witness" was friend of the family's. While this would have worked, the kid that we picked to be the job applicant put the wrong date on the application, screwing up our plan and making the charges stick. Furthermore, there was more trouble to be had and solved because ChiChi was here illegally with an expired visa---so they married her off to one of the tenants, trying to remedy that problem.

THE BUSINESS OF FIRE

Between the years of 1990 and 1993, fire became one of the main sources of my family's income. Being as my mother was, she was never content with just getting a little bit here or there, and once my mom saw what was possible with this tactic, namely arson, she could not be stopped. If it wasn't for that last fire, the state police wouldn't have tracked down Candace's estranged husband Mark, and without tracking him down after one particular fire, it's hard to say how much more time would have gone by before the police raided the house and put an end to the Burt family crime empire. It all had to end eventually, and the fires signaled the beginning of the end.

The last fire, like the others before it, was a grand affair—carefully planned, with every sense of confidence nothing could go wrong. At that time, Mom had moved Rachel into summer house because someone had to take care of Holly, one of the adopted kids, who the state was trying to get back after a series of allegations of sexual, and other forms, of abuse—all of which, of course, were perfectly justified. Anyway, my mom made it clear that in order to keep Holly in the family, Rachel had to be in the summer home to live with her.

I should mention that even after all of that was settled and Holly was with our family to stay, Rachel was still living in the summer house that we had had since we were kids. Mom didn't like that, she had decided that she no longer had any use for that house. Her ambitions, as they so often do, started to climb. She decided that she needed to make room for a bigger structure because of all the grandchildren and as it was, it was only a 3-bedroom ranch.

My mother looked for help from her friend Darcy, who was my mom's go-to lady for all kinds of shady business, especially when it came to handling certain situations. Mom told Darcy it was time to have just one more fire. I do not know who actually lit the match, but with her plans carefully laid out, Mom went to Florida. She brought Rachel in from the summer house to babysit the main house while she was away so that everyone would be out of the way and there'd be no one to worry about, no one to see it, and no one to upset what was going to happen.

Lo and behold, not long after my parents arrived safely in Florida, we got a call informing us the summer house was on fire. Of course, Rachel was ready to have a heart attack about this awful turn of events. No one warned her of anything so all of her worldly possessions, including her wedding pictures as well as other personal items, were gone forever. While she probably should have been grateful that my mother at least bothered to get her out, Mom didn't give Rachel a heads up at all. She just torched it.

When Mom got back she blamed it on Mark because of the grudge she held with him for leaving Candace. Mom lied to the police and said she had information that said Mark was going to do it, so the police went to find Mark in order to get to the bottom of the story.

In a turn of events that even my very forward-thinking mom wouldn't have thought of, Mark flat out told the police he didn't know about that fire in particular or have anything to do with it, adding that he sure knew about some of the other fires that had been set. Before this they were preparing to arrest him for the summer house fire, but he struck a deal to tell them everything in exchange for his ability to walk.

They promised him immunity from any crime he had been involved in and with this, he talked. And talked. And talked.

From those conversations on, the police got the idea that their suspicions about a lot of things had been right all along and they started watching our house non-stop, continuing this surveillance for seven months to a year after Mark spilled the beans.

Part III
The Beginning of the End...

Parental Perspective

It all had to end sometime. I wish it had been sooner, but events took place as they did. I could no longer take the daily horror of life in the Burt family, in the Burt cult. Something had to give. My own children were at risk and I knew what would happen the moment they got old enough to witness some of the horror, the crime, the deception—they would be forever lost to us. And Mom did try to get them turned against us, just like she used to try to turn Arlean and me against one another by setting up "scenes" that would make it look like I was cheating on her or she on me. She would tell my son, little Randy, all the time that his parents did not love him. That they were abusing him, not feeding him, not treating him right. This was the hardest on Arlean, who was already going half crazy making sure the house was as spotless as possible since she felt she was just waiting for the day for Children's Services to come bursting in on my mom's command.

My mother knew that even though Arlean would rail

against her, Arlean couldn't and wouldn't do anything against her because she always had the power of protective services. She led Arlean to live in utter, constant fear of our children being taken away. She used that against her until Arlean was unable to ever relax, to ever feel safe, to ever feel like at any moment her life could be ripped out from beneath her. And for me, my worst fear was not necessarily protective services but the idea that my mother could get custody somehow of our children as we sat helplessly by, living right behind her—near, but far from our children—and watch as they turned against us. Like Nadine's children were taught to beat their own mother, to call her a retard, to hate her—these things all seemed within the realm of possibility at any moment. It was horrifying.

As a parent, a lot of things made me sick to my stomach, more so than they ever could have before having children of my own. The one image that stuck in my mind was the baby boy, Jack, who was Marie's little one. I speculate that because he had a face that looked just like my father's, that my dad had some doing in his conception. My mother hated this baby. From the time it was born, she dismissed it, disliked it, abused it. And this time, especially with a privacy fence that would put the state armory to shame, she was able to get away with far more than she ever could have with us.

Baby Jack's spot, at least when the weather permitted, was right under a tree in the backyard. That's where he was chained for most of the day. Right to a tree. Although it was probably a better place for him to be since my mom would just slap him across his little round face whenever he cried. Marie couldn't ever feed him until she was completely done with the housework so he was hungry, which meant he cried a lot, which meant he got slapped quite often. To try to shut him up, mom would lay him in his bassinet with a bottle propped up on a pillow but it was a long time before the baby could figure out how to get it to his mouth, so he just cried. Everyone wanted to help—wanted to comfort the baby, but if any of us tried to get near him my mom would snap and force us away. As he got older and was chained by the waist to the tree, he started to learn that if he made a sound, he would get hit. For a long time, the only thing you heard out of him was the occasional sniffle or sob.

Because Jack didn't talk (even if it was just out of fear) he was labeled retarded. This is something my mom called all of us growing up and made us feel that we were after being told so often and with physical abuse to accompany it. Jack was abused far worse in some ways than even we were, but despite this she became like a god to him—a fickle one who could either give something (like a little food, for instance) or become instantly savage and rain down punishment without warning. And again, I am forced to think how we all felt growing up with that kind of mind-fucking presence looming. Never knowing—we never knew what could befall us at any moment. So we lived in fear. And like baby Jack, when she told us we were retarded enough times, we didn't question it. We just crouched down like frightened, abused little dogs and submitted to a will that had proved itself to be much stronger and more powerful than our own.

My mom never hugged any of us. She wasn't the type. But for all of his faults and evil deeds, my dad did have a soft spot. And when it came to Jack, he had a really big soft one. There's really no doubt in any of our minds that he was the father and my mom knew this. While she was already just plain cruel to children for pleasure to begin with, this knowledge made her take even greater joy in abusing Jack. She would try to keep my dad away from the baby—all he wanted to do was feed him, hold him, cuddle with him—show him something other than hatred and abuse. And for this, he too was punished.

When you're beaten, kicked down, called retarded and left with nothing to believe in, you'll believe in anything—even if that means accepting that you're a worthless piece of shit. For my mom, this worked like magic for years and years. But it did start to crumble and once it did, it all tumbled down around her.

CONNECTION SEVERED

The day I stopped talking to my family altogether was the day that they beat me within an inch of my life in front my wife and children. The pain was intense but saved me from being part of their sick lives for well over a year—and during that year the police happened to start watching their house, started taking names, and began observing to see who was in the cult and who was out. I was out and for that I was grateful.

We were living in a house behind my parents' sprawling place—always nearby, always within easy distance for them to know everything that was going on, no matter how major or minor. And we were close enough so that when the electric company finally caught on to the fact that my dad had been stealing electric from a rigged box near the house and shut his power off for good, we were close enough that our electric box could serve his purpose and give him power.

The thing is, with my family, it's not like, "Hey, the power's out over here and oh, can I please borrow your power supply and help you pay your bill." It's like my dad storms over without telling anybody, plugs in through our basement, and goes back to his house which is a giant place and probably used more electric in a day than we would in about a month. And furthermore, it's not like he would ever give us a dime for it—and my mother certainly couldn't be counted for on that matter either. At the time, I was doing my best to remain as far away as possible from all of the criminal activity. I had it with that life—for many years prior to that I had been making an honest living working at stores and doing well for myself—at least as well as anyone can do working as an unskilled laborer or in a service job. There was no way in hell we could have just gone ahead and paid their electric bill on our own. We were just getting by as it was.

And so the day that Arlean called me, upset and screaming about my dad stealing our electricity (and knowing we'd be stuck paying for it) I made the decision that I was not going to be walked on any longer. I just was not going to take it. Plain and simple. But I knew it was not going to be easy. You don't say "no" to my parents. And it doesn't matter who you are, if that's something you dare to do, then may the Lord be with you…because no one else will be.

I was determined to do something about it. First though, I had to think about my family. I told Arlean to lock all of the doors and windows and take the kids upstairs. I instructed her to only call the police if someone tried to come inside the house. Then I went to take care of business.

The act was simple. I unplugged their electricity from my house. And all the power went out in theirs. And after that was done, I stepped outside because I knew that something was going to happen and I was going to take what would come. They were not going to be using our electricity and forcing us to pay for it. Sure enough, within a few minutes, Dad came storming over, mad as hell. With a voice that tried to sound collected, he asked nicely—as nice as could be managed. "You have five minutes to hook that back up, Randy." But I didn't.

Sensing something was going down, slowly seven or eight family members started to trickle out of the house, along with my mother. "Four minutes, Randy," my dad said, my mom stood behind him, staring at me hatefully.

Four minutes went by. Suddenly, I was grabbed from behind and held. My mother started slapping and punching me, all while my family watched from the upstairs window. "How about now Randy?" she asked.

I refused.

She made her way over to the series of basement windows and busted out one after the other before moving on to the other windows on our house. At first, she would look to me after a window had been broken, to see if it was having an impact on my decision, I told her, "Go ahead, the insurance will pay for it." Which pissed her off more, and she continued on her rampage.

When she realized that wasn't phasing me, she returned her attention to me.

They weren't used to being told no and then not getting a response to threats. So she did the only thing she thought she could do. She got a big splintery two-by-four piece of wood and started beating me with it. Across my chest, across my strained arms and shoulders, and across my face—over and over in an endless stream of attacks.

She screamed at me, "You rotten piece of shit!" And then took her anger out on the car that Arlean and I owned. It wasn't much, but it was ours, we had worked for it and bought it, legally, and we were proud of it. What's more, the kids loved it. She broke the windows, beat the hell out of it like it was one of her kids.

At some point, she returned to me and beat me and beat me and only left me there when they were worried they'd actually gone and done it this time and killed me.

Of course, I wasn't dead. I was definitely wounded and I stuck to my resolve. That electricity did not stay plugged in. In exchange, we were denied the "privilege" of speaking with them from that point until the raid. In my eyes, and in Arlean's, this couldn't be seen as anything other than a blessing.

When they left me bloody and broken, stomped on by other members of the family who decided to help my mom, a slow thought came to my clouded, bruised head. These people were evil and the less we had to do with them the better off we'd be. With a broken arm and more bruises than I could ever count—with a screaming, crying wife and children so upset they could not catch their breath—with all of this I was determined to build back up. Get a new car. Fix the house. Heal my damaged body... Move on. Somehow. Somehow then I knew it would happen. And it was this day that was the last day that I ever had any contact with my family.

My parents got their electricity elsewhere, probably from one of my other brother's houses, and wrote us off completely. I didn't consider it a loss.

JUSTICE ASLEEP AT THE WHEEL...

Although I don't talk to them any longer, with the exception of Rachel and some other people who are a bit farther removed, my family is still doing the same thing they've been doing for years and years—stealing, lying, and trying to get the most out of everyone they possibly can. I know they continue to commit these crimes because I know their techniques and I have viewed what still goes on. The internet has made it possible for me to keep some tabs on members of my family I don't speak to and the more I see of what's been going on since they've been out of the slammer, the more I am disheartened with the justice system. Not long ago, I saw evidence of a lavish party my parents threw, complete with hired hula dancers and what looked like plenty of food and drinks for an army. Furthermore, the control over the Carpenter's is still there as I saw Luke in a picture that had been taken at one of their parties.

How is this even possible? I am sure you're wondering how two people who owe hundreds of thousands of dollars to the state of Rhode Island could afford to do anything but wait to die so they'll be forgiven of their debt... Well, let me tell you.

Not only do they owe the state money, but they owe even more to companies and individuals for restitution. It's my opinion that the stupid state doesn't realize what's going on and has decided it's fine with them to take teeny tiny payments from the Burts, who have claimed to be poor. Everyone knows they have plenty of money. Sure, they'll never have quite the empire they used to, but they aren't hurting. The little payments they make to "make things right" are a joke. Furthermore, the state is getting screwed in a less direct way. Somehow my parents were never charged with tax fraud, although I'm sure even a quick inspection of their records would reveal some nasty surprises if anyone would just bother to look. Even from the time we were young, Mom would commit tax fraud every year, doing little things like making up a boatload of receipts from companies that didn't even exist to "pay for" work that she had all of her kids doing for her for free. She wrote off our efforts on the apartments for years. And she'd always find an excuse if she got audited. For instance, when the summer house went up in flames, all she did was say that her receipts had been in the house...how convenient that fire was for her. The number of tax documents she faked would have astounded any auditor who actually took the time to investigate. She'd go so far as to have fake letterhead and other documents made for these invisible companies who were doing work for her. She had companies like the one my uncle owned give her even more false documentation saying they did thousands of dollars in work for her and of course, none of that really happened either. How is it possible in a justice system that claims to be the best in the world, that this woman and her husband walk free? I don't understand why the state and the federal government wouldn't work to connect the dots back to when they were taking income when their kids were doing work for them, keeping the difference and not reporting it to a tax authority?

Ever since the fire that sparked the police's interest through talking to Candace's ex-husband, Mark—who proceeded to tell them everything in the world he knew about what the Burts had been up to for so many years, the police set about watching the house like hawks. They took careful note of who came and went, and over time, it became clear to them that I had nothing to do with them. Sure, I lived right behind their house. Sure, I was family and sometimes we'd drive past one another—but for all intents and purposes, they were nothing to us and we made it clear that we were nothing to them either. There was simply no contact and yes, as you might imagine, this led to some tense living conditions but what could we do? After we ceased to have contact with them, we were barely making ends meet. We were living off my salary and barely making it, it was a very hard time.

*   *   *   *   *

THE UNRAVELING

I will never forget the morning it all happened and the recount that I am about to tell is the way the day really went down.

It was 5:00 in the morning when I was abruptly awoken by yelling and noise that was coming from outside the house towards my family's home. I remember at first thinking, "What the hell is going on?" and immediately jumping to the conclusion that it had to be some level of craziness that was happening with my family. Remember, very little that they did surprised me; it could have been any number of things happening at that moment.

I got dressed quickly, looking out the window the entire time. At that point, I could see towards my mother's house, which was surrounded by a tall row of hedges. In the dim morning light, I could see something happening, a fight of some kind or another, on the back porch of the house. I couldn't make out who it was, whether it was my dad, or Bruce, or anyone else, so I went downstairs to the back deck to see if I could get a better view.

At this point, I had not been over to my parent's house in almost a year and I was not "in the loop" with anything that was going on, or what they were up to. Although it was safe to assume that they were still up to their old tricks.

When I got downstairs and outside, there was a part of me that just wanted to say, "Screw it," and head back up to bed, however, curiosity got the better of me.

Suddenly, Trisha came running away from the house like she was on fire, heading directly for her house which was caddy -corner from the others. Recognizing her, while also realizing that something major was occurring, I yelled to her, "What's happening?!"

She looked at me with crazed eyes, like the devil had come to collect his due and screamed, "Everyone is under arrest! They are arresting everyone! I need to call the lawyer!"

My mind reeled. "What are you talking about? What the hell is happening?" I screamed. It was like I was moving in slow motion.

"It's the police! They're here!" She continued off in a sprint.

I stood there for a moment open mouthed, "What the hell is this?" and then collected my wits enough to finally re-focus my eyes and realize that police officers were surrounding the house. With Arlean looking from the windows of our home, and me there in the yard, state police, local police swarmed around the house, their cars parked everywhere. I stood there watching in amazement. It was like something you saw on TV.

I went in the house and joined Arlean by the window. She looked up at me with questions in her eyes and I shrugged my shoulders, "I have no idea, it's none of my business. I'm not involved in this shit. I don't want to be involved." However, even though I had a casual demeanor on the exterior, inside I felt the first prickling of panic. I wondered, "Are they going to come for me too?" Sure, I had been separated for a year, but that didn't mean I wasn't implicated in anything from the past.

We continued to watch and the nerves slowly exhibited themselves. Arlean and I paced, back and forth, looking out the windows, running our hands through our hair.

Finally, our vigil was interrupted by Trisha. She came to the house, knocked on the door, and we answered. We let her in.

Whatever was going on, while it didn't offer itself to make a would-be truce between us, still connected us out of sheer desire to learn our fate.

Trisha, suffice to say, was a mess. She started going on and on, and we listened, quietly, gauging all of it for insight as to what would happen next.

"They arrested everyone, Raymond, everyone. I don't know what to do." And we didn't know what to tell her. Suddenly, another harsh knock sounded at the door and the three of us nearly jumped out of our skin.

"This can't be good," I'm thinking to myself, half expecting to go open the door and be met with my own set of handcuffs and a round of police. All of us started to scatter into different rooms, out of our own fear and half not knowing if they would have a warrant. Arlean tentatively opened the door and instead of the cops, it was a disheveled, tear-stained Holly. "Hide me! They're gonna take me like they took everybody else" she pled, searching my eyes for any signs of weakness. At that point in time, she wasn't more than eleven years old, but she was still not my favorite person in the world. Holly was the product of my father raping Nadine. My mother wanted yet another daughter prior to Holly's birth, but since my mom had had her tubes tied, she decided she could get her wish if Nadine produced offspring by way of my father. Once Holly was born, she was adopted by my mother and treated as her own.

Personally, I thought she was a spoiled brat who got everything she wanted. She knew she'd have a hard time convincing me to give her relief from the cops. Part of me was about to tell her to get out because I didn't think it was worth it to try to save her at the risk of being involved. However, then she appealed to me in a way that I could not refuse her. Even though the news was being delivered by her, I had to have compassion.

She said, "They arrested Mom and Dad and everyone and they are taking all of kids. The cops said that they were going to send all of us to the state!"

I swallowed hard, this meant all of my nieces and nephews, would be sent somewhere else. The only thing they had been guilty of was being born to the wrong family and I couldn't allow this to happen.

With this news, I set my jaw and decided that something had to be done. I told her to stay in the house and walked out the door. I walked around my mother's house, taking the long way, because I didn't want to go directly in the backdoor. When I rounded the corner and faced my mother's house, I caught my breath. There must have been at least twenty police cars parked on the street, along with a few crime scene vans. There were crowds of people all over the street, onlookers galore you would have thought a parade was about to come down the street. However, what I noted above all things was the fact that it was quickly becoming a media circus....there were dozens of reporters and news vans there. It was staggering.

I neared the yellow police tape and observed men in suits going in and out of the house. Separating myself from the crowd, I crossed the police line and went toward the front door, which was misshapen and dented from being the target of the battering ram during the raid.

Observing the broken lock that hung dejectedly from the door, I remember thinking, "Oh hell, this is so not good."

When I got inside, the first thing that struck me was that all the teenagers were there, facedown against the couch, with their hands cuffed behind them. They all looked scared shitless and tired. My nieces and nephews were screaming and crying for me, confused and terrified. It was absolutely heart wrenching to listen to. Rachel and some of the other adults were nearby, sitting on their knees with their hands locked behind their backs. No one said a word to me. There was loud crashing from other parts of the house as the police were tearing the upstairs apart.

I am beyond asking questions at this point—I see clearly what's happened but am worried to death about what is going to become of the kids. In my mind, I had every reason to hate my family—to never speak to them again, but when it came to my nieces and nephews, I had nothing but love and concern. They, like me or any of the other kids who grew up in the Burt family, had no choice but to be a Burt. They were innocent, they'd been through enough. I would have done anything in the world at that moment to just be able to pick them up all at once in my arms and dash out of the house to somewhere safe— somewhere far away from the never-ending drama.

It was at this point that I was finally addressed. "Oh well look what we have here...another visitor...who are you?" said a cop who suddenly emerged into my line of site.

"Randy Burt," I replied, steeling myself for the worst.

The cop looked pleased. "Oh good, another Burt," he said sarcastically. He took his handcuffs off his belt as he yelled, "Do we have a 'Randy Burt' on that list?"

I was fully expecting to be cuffed and arrested at that point. However, a plainclothes detective joined our conversation, looking at a pad of paper that clearly had the names of who needed to be brought in during this raid. He flipped through the pad and looked up at us, "No, he's not on this list. However, I need to speak to you. I have a note that we need to talk. Sit over there." He pointed to a couch and felt my stomach release of some of its panic and anxiety. He wasn't done talking. "Do not move. Do not touch anything. Do not talk to anyone until I return."

I nodded. You can be damn sure I was going to follow the rules.

I sat down and watched what was happening. The cops were leaving no stone unturned, no drawer untouched. Every-thing—and I mean everything, has been either destroyed, top-pled, broken, smashed, or thrown aside. There is no doubt that they were looking for something everywhere they could possi-bly look. In fact, long after the raid a private investor took back ownership on the property and gave it to the city so it could be searched fully. The guy ended up bulldozing the place looking for buried money or a safe—the more dirt the police could on the Burts, the happier they were. And truth be told, I think they were just thrilled to have the opportunity to barge in and trash a house as fine as that one was. I hadn't been in it for one hell of long time, but I knew that there was a lot of valuable stuff in it—and they were making sure all of it was found.

I noted with interest that they seemed to also be on to my mom's tricks. Not only going for the obvious of dumping out drawers and searching closets, they were tapping the walls. Seems to me, they knew that my mother had false walls in the place.

I heard a cop instructing another officer. "When you search, make sure you do it well. A simple shelf like this," he motioned to a shelf in a bookcase, sweeping it thoroughly, "produces this." He produced a man's wallet, stuffed with money. "They have stuff stashed all over the house just like this. Don't gloss over anything."

Finally, attention was turned to me. A couple of cops, one of whom I found out later was named Sergeant Pendergrass, came to get me. I noticed they didn't seem to want to handcuff me or push me around, which was a good sign. We went off to a private room away from my family members being held and from the noise of the raid going in full force. "Look," says Pendergrass, "we know you're not a bad guy. No one has said a single bad thing about you. You don't come up at all in our investigations and we also know that you haven't talked to any of these bastards in about a year. You're not in trouble as far as we're concerned here."

I took a breath, again, hardly believing my good fortune. Pendergrass continued. "However, we know that you know what's been going on over here though—and we're going to have to have you testify. You need to tell me everything, what has gone down, when, where, you need to spill it."

I stared at the floor as he spoke. "Listen," I said. "I haven't spoken to any of them in a year, I haven't stepped foot in this house in a year. I don't know how much help I can offer. I am here because of my nieces and nephews. I don't want them to go to the state. I can't let that happen. I want to take them all with me."

Pendergrass shook his head. "I'm sorry Randy, I can't allow that. They have to go to state care. I don't want to alarm you, but if you don't want to cooperate with us, I am going to make your life very difficult."

"I can't do this," I said. "You guys don't understand. People have gone after my mom, trying to put her in jail before, and it never worked. And if I have to testify against my mom, and she doesn't go to jail forever, I live right next door and you have no idea what would happen to me."

Pendergrass shook his head yet again. "Randy, your mother is going to *die* in prison. Do you understand? She is never going to get out. She has seen her last day of freedom, today. She is in custody right now and she is never going to be free again in her life. Never. You have a chance to help us."

I steeled myself, still not fully believing his words. "I need to think about this," I conceded, I couldn't give him anything more at that point. "I need to talk to my wife. This isn't just about me." Even though the thought of my mother rotting in prison made me feel almost giddy with excitement, I still didn't want to be overly optimistic and I didn't know if I could testify. Risks, guilt, fear, all of these made me want to run, there was so much involved.

He nodded. "You do that, I'll be in touch. You are free to go."

I turned around, returning home, wanting to clear my head and talk this all over with Arlean. I was emotionally and mentally exhausted.

When I entered my house, I filled Arlean in on all the details. I noted with interest that Holly was still there, and so was Rachel's son. I felt as if I had a small victory, at least two of the kids were out.

It was then that another hammering knock sounded at the door. It was Pendergrass again. I swallowed hard. What now?

"You have two of those kids in here, don't you?"

I stared at him blankly, employing my best poker face.

"Look Randy. If you do not give us those kids, we are going to arrest you and your wife and we are going to take your kids from you. If you don't turn them over, we will get a warrant for you both and your kids will end up as wards of the state."

I shook my head and called to Arlean to get Rachel's son and Holly, I wasn't going to make more problems. Just turn them over and then figure all of this out.

It was at about 2:30 or 3:00 pm that day that my family decided it was time to reconnect with me, the prodigal son. They all wanted information from me. I got a call from my dad who told me I needed to flush a stash of cocaine that he had hidden and was using to pay off people. For some reason I did this and told the cops later that I did.

Then, my mother rang. She started her diatribe out saying how much she loved me and needed my help. She said that I shouldn't talk to the police and that she needed me to handle things for her until a lawyer was able to straighten all of this out.

Even from within prison, she was still trying to manipulate us. This was after a year of not talking to either Arlean or I. This was after the last time we had contact, when she beat me within an inch of my life with a two by four.

I hung up the phone. I told Arlean, "After everything, now she tells us she loves us? What a joke."

The next day, they came to my house again and reiterated their message and added some interesting caveats to the situation. They said they knew that Arlean had been overpaid in welfare, they said they knew that we had committed welfare fraud and if I didn't talk, they would arrest us on that charge and take our kids and put them in children's protective services. However, they added, if I cooperated, they would pretend that the welfare fraud never happened.

That was it—they knew how important our children were to us and they knew that that was the one thing they could do to get us to turn over.

And that was that...the beginning of the end of everything. For us, for them—or better yet, it was the beginning of a new start for us.

But of course, before all of that, we had a lot of work to do and a lot to face up to.

COMING CLEAN

A strange thing happened when the reality that we might lose our children began to sink in—the reality of everything started to hit too. The reality that for so long we'd been living in a prison already, the only difference was that we could come and go. That was the prison that my mother and her years of twisted lies and manipulations built but for the first time, even if it took such drastic measures, we saw an escape route. The day I told Arlean to forget about protecting anyone in the family and keep the kids safe, was the first day of the rest of my life—the life I've been living from that moment on has been real, the one before it was so contorted that in many ways, it should never counted as a life except in name. It was no way to exist.

There was a lot to be done, of course, before we would be free from my family's stranglehold and the cops knew that they found our weak spot—our children. I was also concerned for my nieces and nephews who like me and my brothers and sisters, whether biological or not, never deserved to be caught up in such a web in the first place. I will never forget the look on their faces that day that they were lined up in the house where their grandmother lived like little criminals. Their eyes were so wide. They looked so helpless and confused. Their entire world was being ripped apart and they could hear and see it happening.

"We don't want to arrest you...we don't want any of this for you. We just want, need, you to testify." The reason they needed us so badly was because my parents' lawyer had been making people like Nadine and Luke, as well as some of the other kids, take mental competency tests. They had all failed and could not be used as reliable witnesses by the prosecution. Therefore, on that one technicality, they could have gotten off because of this manipulation by the defense. So we agreed to it.

The prosecutor and others there knew that they were going to get the information they needed from me. They had all but seen me turn over before their eyes at the threat of losing the kids. I think they were less worried and more willing to work with me. When I asked them about Trisha's four children, I was definitely worried. I knew that Trisha couldn't bail herself out because she couldn't prove that her money had been made legally. I pleaded with them, that the kids were innocent victims in what they were damn well aware of being a lot of crime perpetuated by their grandmother. I said, "Let me pay Trisha's bail. Please. It's my own money—I've worked for it, you guys know that. Just please let me help those kids by getting Trisha out so they can be with her. They've been through so much shit, you have to understand."

At first they hesitated, telling me that if I tried to pay anyone's bail I'd be spending one hell of a lot of time in jail. And then they really started working me, making sure I was on their side. And do you know what? I was on their side. Heart and soul—there was no more looking back for me. I was ready to move on, surge forward, no matter what it might mean.

I looked them in the eye, took a deep breath, and said, "I want my children and my nieces and nephews—every single one of them—placed in my care immediately...Do that, and do it now, and I am yours. I will tell you anything and everything you need to know. You have my solemn word. I am ready for this."

And that same night they brought them all to my house. Those frightened, confused kids—all at my home, all wondering what in the hell they had done to deserve such a thing; what their parents had done to be taken away by the police. It was hell, but at least they were safe. At least they would never go through what any of my brothers and sisters who had been handed over went through. No torture, no abuse, no manipulating—they had their lives in front of them and even though I felt like my world was crumbling, this kept me strong. For the first time in a long time I felt like I was doing exactly what I was supposed to be doing. And it was the right thing to do.

But while coming clean on the welfare fraud and facing those charges was a difficult time, the real challenge was ahead of us. It was when the questions started coming in, rolling in with threats, veiled and real, about what our coming clean might mean. In no time after we'd been back home the questions started, "So how is that you guys managed to get out when everyone else went down?" It didn't take any kind of super sleuth ability to figure out what was going on. Besides, it was hardly a secret that I wasn't what you'd call "on friendly terms" with my family to begin with.

So I made a deal and it was the first day of the rest of our lives.

However, the moment I did, my entire family turned on one another, like sharks after the same piece of meat. Raymond wanted me to get him a deal. The cops said they would if he turned in evidence of a homicide Dennis had committed. However, to do this Raymond wanted me to implicate myself in planting a gun and saying it was the murder weapon. I refused to do this and allowed them to continue on, all eager to see one another out.

The cops wanted Arlean and I to get in touch with Arlean's parents, they wanted us to be somewhere safe. Now, we had not seen her parents in over twenty years, Arlean didn't even know if they were alive. However, the police tracked them down and told them to expect a call from us.

This was something that we would have never been allowed to get away with before. For years Arlean had wanted to do this—to run to them, to know them once again, but although it might be hard for anyone outside of my family to believe, this was completely impossible. I can't make it clear enough how we were like prisoners in my mom's family. And now that we were free, we knew we had some living and some real catching up to do.

When people ask me why we didn't leave earlier than that time when it crumbled, I have a hard time explaining—not because I don't know or understand, but because it's just way too complex to rehash in a short conversation. There are no simple answers to any questions about my family, just as there are no answers to questions about other cults. People always just want to know, "Yes, but you knew things were getting scary and it's not like they were locking you up to keep you there, so what is the real reason you stayed?" I don't know if this book, this confession, this outpouring of memories, regrets, and crushing pain from my youth until now really answers it still, but I think it is a start.

I think Arlean tells it best. When she was initially questioned by the police, they pulled her into a separate room and they asked her, "Why did you never leave? Why did you never try to escape? To contact your parents?"

Crying, she simply replied, "Because I love Randy, because I love my kids." When they took us to the station, they took Arlean in first. I had given her a nod, as if to say, "Say whatever you want." And she did.

Privately, they asked Arlean. "So tell us about Frances."

She said, "Well, she's a royal BITCH, but what else do you want to know?" The officer questioning her started to name off other names, if she had heard of these people and admitted who she had heard of and who she had not. She talked about individual crimes she had been made to commit, she told them about the shoplifting schemes and everything else she knew.

Finally, when they talked to me, I told them whatever I knew. I stayed factual, only stating what I knew exactly about or what I had seen. I confirmed the acts of arson, I confirmed the shoplifting, I confirmed stealing the furniture of tenants, everything that we did, I confirmed it with the police.

The only way out of my family was death or life in prison. I just remember Darcy, who was a member of the Burt cult since she'd seen one hell of lot on the dirty-job end of my mom's schemes, crying and hugging me when my parents went to jail. This same woman who was ready to kill herself because she knew she knew too much. This same woman who, like Nadine had been pressed into owing my mom a little bit at first and then her life by the end after manipulation after gruesome manipulation, cried and said, "This is the only way it ever could have ended, Randy." And still, I don't think she ever felt free. She can't just like we can't.

We did try, and damned if I know how to tell you this with the words that fall so flat as I write them. We did try. We did want out. We lived in a state of agonizing dependence because that is the way she designed everything. When I got in a car accident and got a large settlement and Arlean and I could finally look one another in the eyes and say, "Here it is. Here is our one chance to get out. To take our kids and go somewhere else," it was all stopped. My mother wouldn't let us move and turned very generous, admitting that our family was crammed into a small house. She contracted Raymond to make our own house much bigger, nicer—she made it seem like she'd finally come around, begun to love us. And guess what? After a lifetime of falling for this, we fell for it again. And for what it's worth, those modifications to make our house bigger and better never happened, or at least were never completed. Raymond of course did some of the work, got paid for the entire job, and left it unfinished, but that didn't matter. The whole purpose was just to get us to stay anyway, why would it matter if the job was done correctly to anyone else?

We wanted so much more for our lives. And when I say "more" I don't mean more house room to live in, more money to spend, or more gifts for the ridiculously evil Christmas crime -fest either. We wanted more love to share with our children, more room to think as individuals, more space to grow apart from the torment of years and years. But it just couldn't happen by itself. When we lived behind my mother, we weren't even allowed to have our own telephone. In my mother's mind, if something was important enough to warrant a phone call, then we could certainly be inspired enough to walk over to her house, now couldn't we?

Like any former cult member will tell you, what sound most simple—what seems most obvious—is sometimes the most impossible.

The Prosecution Rests

What was especially brilliant about the court case, when it did happen, was that the prosecutor was one straight shooter. Of course, all of the members of my family had "lawyered up" and were all presented in court in front of the public and the media circus that had been generated by this point in time.

The prosecutor didn't argue that any of my family couldn't have bail set. He didn't insist upon them staying in jail. Instead he said that bail couldn't get posted with money that was made by ill-gotten means and that they had to prove that the money that was posted for them was from legitimate means.

To be expected, this was hard for them.

Of course, while they might have had their own set of problems. It wasn't as easy for Arlean and I to just start talking and be done with all of them. Of course, we had to disassociate ourselves from them and this was in everything, down to the property that we owned, to our bank accounts. We had to untangle ourselves from the Burts in order to move on with our life.

This included getting my parents to sign off on a quit claim deed for our house, as my name, as well as the name of my mother and father were on the property. This was done easily enough and it was done at the right time, with my parents both signing the paperwork with my lawyer from a jail cell.

However, soon thereafter, it started to surface that I had made a deal with the prosecution and this news trickled back to my mother. Admittedly, she was furious, out of her mind mad.

She called my lawyer from the jail, screaming at him that she changed her mind. That she did not want the quit claim deed recorded with her signature. So, when I went down to pick up the deed, the lawyer said he couldn't give it to me because of her phone call. I reminded him that he worked for me and that if she signed the document, that should be it, end of story.

Unfortunately, my lawyer said that it doesn't work that way and that he couldn't record the deed because of my mother's late refusal after she had signed the document. Because of this, the deed was never filed and Arlean and I lost our house.

It was then that we decided to leave Rhode Island and we thought in order to be safe, we needed to move. Far away. Arlean's parents were living in the South. That's where we decided to go.

GETTING OUT ALIVE

Arlean and I made it out alive. Our children made it out somewhat unscathed; untainted. But many others in my family were never able to fully recover. And by "my family" I don't just mean my biological brothers and sisters—I mean anyone who ended up locked into our lives by force of will stronger than could beat.

And while we are alive and physically healthy, we are not

well entirely. We never will be. We do not trust anyone—we cannot. Furthermore, Arlean and I just do not feel comfortable in public, I don't know if we ever will. While we are out and away from a life of torture and manipulate, we are left to torture ourselves with our memories and guilt and manipulate our own selves into thinking that we are going to be okay always. Because so often, so much is on shaky ground when we look back and it seems that the older we get, the more we see the innocence of our grandchildren, the more we understand just how dark our pasts were.

We have taught our kids that their family is me, Arlean, and Arlean's parents. They know that none of my family is considered, or ever will be considered, family.

I don't sleep. I just cannot. The memories and thoughts that keep me wide awake, that make me toss and turn one sleepless night after another are not even specific any longer—the memories that haunt me are so numerous that they are just a vague black mass that sits over me, that hovers, that pulls my eyes open from sleep.

When the vastly incorrect portrayal of my family in the made for television movie "Family Sins" came out, it reopened sores that had remained closed. So much of it was off-base, only keeping with the basic facts of the case, but it wasn't that that drove me to the brink. It was that those wounds were because my children were suffering. My daughter received emails asking her how her family could do such a thing; asking her what kind of evil, sick, heartless people she came from. She couldn't respond to those emails no matter how much they upset her because she didn't remember any of this. She wasn't even around when the worst of it was going full swing.

All my daughter knew was that she had been raised in a happy home with a mom and dad who were still in love, so much, that it looked like teenage puppy love, making her want to gag, and with brothers and a sister who were fun to be around and who loved to joke and mess with her. She knew happiness. She knew only what is normal for a kid her age in America to know. She knew a few things about the family's past, but like my other kids, knew better than to make it the topic of conversation.

And now, with grandchildren and the slowing down of age, I want to give an answer. I want her to be able to send the full text of this very book in response to an email. Because she is not qualified to answer. She is innocent—we were all innocent when we were young. We were abused so badly, made to feel so small, so worthless, that all we knew was that we needed to belong, to be accepted, to get by. But we were also trained to believe we could not get by without Queen Frances. These are questions no one can answer except for those who were there— those who felt the sting of the electrical cord daily as it ripped into the flesh, those whose heads were forced into toilets, those who were told they were retarded (despite vast intelligence) so long that they had nothing else to believe.

Of course, we all know that my mother and father are out of jail; that original cop wasn't able to make good on the idea that she would die in jail. However, I am dead to my family. And that's fine with me. I want nothing to do with them.

However, I know I am still on their radar.

As I was writing this book, while I am incredibly grateful for the outpouring of support from people I know and people I don't, I was also very vocal that I was going to tell my side of the story and news traveled. My mother went so far as to find out the name and phone number of my editor and called to scream at her about how I was the bad guy, that it had been me all along who perpetuated everything, it had been all my idea and that she was an innocent woman, never committing a crime in her life. She said that she had never stolen anything, had never done anything wrong, that it was everyone else, not her. My editor, after listening for a moment and then stating that she worked for Randy and for the publisher and not Frances Burt, wisely hung up on my mother.

Another family member (I am sure of it, even though they gave a different name on the phone) called my publisher, the president of the company himself, issuing a string of threats against him. My publisher assured the person on the phone that I had every right to print this book, as we were only going to be talking about the charges that were pled guilty to and the convictions that were doled out. Then he too, hung up.

Furthermore, my family had hounded me and attacked me online, posting messages through my blog and working their hardest to derail interest and defame me. I have tried not to let this bother me and I wonder if they realized that in their efforts to get the book stopped and to throw me under the bus, they were actually just generating more drama and inevitably more interest by their efforts? I wonder if I should actually thank them for creating such a buzz about the book prior to publication?

My family may still be out there, and they may still be pissed off at me. That's fine. I am followed by my family history enough. They will not dictate the course of my future, and I will not allow them to be an ever present specter in my children's or grandchildren's lives. My kids are a hundred, thousand, a million times better than my family, and I won't let anyone tell them different.

I want my children and their children and the kids who come after them to know these things. Those future generations who know somewhere in their lineage are members of their own family who were so remarkably bad and evil that a movie was made about them and a book was written—I want them to understand, to feel. To grasp and to realize what happens when truly evil adults brainwash and mentally drain children. I was a product of that. My brothers and sisters—biological and adopted—are products of that. We are all tainted, soiled, dirty from this and it's a stain we'll never wash away.

I want to have faith in the system of justice we live under but I cannot. I hope the world that my future descendents encounter does not offer such a stark, sad route to achieving what is right.

I want to have faith in the power of forgiveness just as much, and I do. I can forgive myself only because I know I will never forget the horror of our lives and that which we inflicted on others. I can forgive myself because I know that I am so profoundly sorry that there are no words of apology that exist that can be up to the task of even asking for forgiveness.

I want to have faith in the cleansing power of release through confession and revelation and now I do.

*   *   *   *   *

I AM RANDY BURT. This has been my story.

Not my children's story and not their children's story. My own story. Because the evil and filth—the dark empire led by my mother—is over.

A new day has begun. And it is so much brighter than anything I have ever seen before.

Acknowledgements

I would like to thank my publisher, Phillip Vera of EDGE Publishing Company with the help he has provided me in getting this book to press. I know it has been an involved process, but I appreciate you for believing in me and my story. Thank you to my editor, Amanda Clark, for your help in arranging and directing me through the publishing process. Thank you to Sadie E. Nezich my cover designer, I appreciate your creativity and your inspiration.

I have learned a few things about myself and people since I started writing this book. I always felt growing up that I was dumb, that I was a burden on my family, largely because that's how my family made me feel. I was taught at an early age to lie, cheat and steal. I was whipped, beat, made to feel like a nobody. I was lucky I had a few people in my life that took the time to show me I was better than that.

I think there are a lot of people who struggle everyday with abuse, whether it's a child, an adult or an elderly individual. After years of dealing with my past, I can finally say I will no longer let it define me. I urge everyone to understand that if you are made to feel less than worthy, hit or beat up, or threatened or terrorized about the thought of getting out or leaving, please get help, you are worth so much and you do not deserve the pain and suffering you are going through. Seek out a close friend, a teacher or anyone you feel comfortable with.

I believe we all are born with a sense of right and wrong. As a small baby we are filled with joy and love and as we grow it is up to the family and friends around us to guide and nurture that sense of good. But far too many times there are people like my parents who think children are tools of the trade and teach us to be corrupt or abuse us into performing the way they want us to. However it happens, that good is always inside us even though it might be buried or we might be trained to forget about it. However, I know it is always there. You just have to get around the roadblocks that are standing in your way of being the person you are meant to be. Take it from me, I know you can do it. So in ending I encourage you to call for help as well as to report an abusive situation. Don't wait till it's too late.

Resources

Childabuse.com
www.childabuse.com
1-800-4-A-CHILD

Safe Horizon
www.safehorizon.org
1-800-621-HOPE (Domestic Violence)
1-212-227-3000 (Rape, Sexual Assault, & Incest)

Office for Victims of Crime
www.ojp.usdoj.gov
1-800-799-SAFE (Domestic Violence)
1-800-4-A-CHILD (Child Abuse)

The National Domestic Violence Hotline
www.ndvh.org
1-800-799-SAFE (Domestic Violence)

About the Author

Randy Burt is the third oldest biological son born to Walter and Frances Burt. He grew up in Pawtucket, Rhode Island where he lived in a house that saw much despair and suffering and witnessed many crimes, to which he found himself somewhat of a reluctant accomplice for close to 30 years. However, today he knows hope. After being instrumental in the downfall of his family's crime ring, he once again calls Rhode Island home and is coming to grips with his past. He is happily married to his wife Arlean and is surrounded by his five children and seven grandchildren. His kids only know a happy home life, and he intends to keep it that way.